CAVE OF FEAR

By Don Wulffson

An RGA Book

PRICE STERN SLOAN
Los Angeles

Published by Price Stern Sloan, Inc.,
A member of the Putnam & Grosset Group,
New York, New York.

ISBN 0-8431-3861-0
First Edition
10 9 8 7 6 5 4 3 2 1

Library of Congress Cataloging-in-Publication Data

Wulffson, Don L.
Cave of Fear / by Don Wulffson.
p. cm. — (Nightmares! How will yours end?)
"An RGA book."
Summary: While on a camping trip, the reader gets lost in a cave and makes choices which determine the story's outcome.
ISBN 0-8431-3861-0
[1. Plot-your-own stories. 2. Caves—Fiction. 3. Camping—Fiction. 4. Plot-your-own stories.] I. Title. II. Series: Wulffson, Don L. Nightmares! How will yours end?
PZ7.W96373Cav 1994
[Fic]—dc20 94-22679
CIP
AC

COVER ILLUSTRATION BY MIA TAVONATTI.
INTERIOR ICON ILLUSTRATIONS BY NEAL YAMAMOTO.

For Charles R. Wulffsohn, my father, my best friend, and the finest man I've ever known

—D. W.

How Your Nightmare Works

Try to stay awake—you won't want to miss any of the exciting endings in *Cave of Fear*! Each ending is different, and it's up to you to decide your fate. Most of the endings are nightmarish . . . but if you're lucky, you will find yourself back on the path to reality. When you meet a woman dressed as a little girl, should you stay and play with her, or does her friendliness seem a little unnatural? Will you take Mr. Skalaka's offer to learn about your future, or will you resist the temptation to cheat time? The choice is yours. Here's how it works:

First turn to the next page and learn where your nightmare takes place. Read on and find out which friends will be joining you. Then your adventure begins. Your goal is to find your way out of the Cave of Fear and back to your grandfather, with whom you are vacationing in the Transylvanian Alps.

It's easy, it's fun, and it's very, very scary. Just read to the end of each section and follow the directions. You will be offered a choice of pages to turn to, or else instructed to simply go to the next page. And what happens when you reach the ending of one story? Why, just go back, make a different decision, and take a whole new frightening route!

Ready to begin? Good luck . . . and **Sweet Dreams!**

The Setting

You and your grandfather are taking a vacation in Romania, the place of his birth. While there, you meet three other Americans, Caroline Meyers and her children, Tanya and Shawn. One day, on a picnic, your grandfather tells the story of Vlad Tepes (otherwise known as Dracula), and Countess Nadasy, the original vampires.

Full from a sumptuous lunch, you doze off . . . but you never would have allowed yourself the doubtful luxury of sleep had you known what nightmarish events lay ahead of you.

Close to your picnic spot looms a gigantic mountain. While you rest, you dream about a monstrous bat whose mouth forms the entrance to the Cave of Fear. That is where your nightmare takes place. You enter the cave, realizing that Tanya and Shawn are there, too.

As the three of you search for a way out of the cave and back to safety, death and danger await around every corner. Feeling your way along slimy walls, down darkened tunnels, and through pools of putrid water, you run from all kinds of horrific creatures, including vampires, bats, and ghosts, in a perilous attempt to reach your families.

The Cave of Fear can trick you. At times it allows

you to think you have reached the outside in safety —only to discover it is an illusion, and the *real* nightmare has only just begun. But whatever happens in this world of dreams, it is guaranteed to be exciting, unpredictable, and totally petrifying!

Cast of Characters

Shawn Meyers, 15, is the son of the family that you and your grandfather meet while on vacation. His bulging muscles and unkempt reddish-brown hair cause him to look a little like a rebel, but he is actually good-natured and considerate.

Tanya Meyers, 14, shares her brother's friendly disposition, as well as his good looks. Her dark green eyes, honey-colored hair, and flawless skin make her one of the prettiest girls you have ever met. Although she is usually unassuming, there are times when she can be assertive and quite impulsive.

Caroline Meyers, their mother, reminds you a little of your own. She is caring and likeable, and you can see where Tanya and Shawn acquired their own favorable traits. Mrs. Meyers also seems to be responsible, and you would trust her to take control in a dangerous situation.

Your grandfather, who has a gift for storytelling, has taken you to Romania while your parents are on their second honeymoon. He is relaxed and happy to be back in his homeland and is eager to share its history with you, as well as his own.

Your mom and dad are on their second honeymoon, so you go on a trip with your grandfather to Romania, the place of his birth. In the town of Adjud you strike up a friendship with three other American travelers, Caroline Meyers and her two kids, Tanya and Shawn, both close to your age.

One evening, while having dinner with your new friends at a sidewalk café, Tanya and her mom come up with the idea of going on a picnic with you and your grandfather. By the time dinner is finished, plans are made to go the following day.

The next morning, your grandfather rents an odd, oversized foreign car. After stocking it with blankets, baskets of food, sunscreen, and everything else imaginable, you set off on an outing that will take you up into the Transylvanian Alps.

Sitting in the spacious backseat, you feel totally at ease with Shawn and Tanya. Shawn, 15, is the oldest, and though he is a quiet, gentle person, he looks fearsome. Big for his age, his muscular build shows off his love for weightlifting. But his reddish-brown hair, which he wears long and which makes him look like he needs a haircut, gives him a bit of a rebel look. Tanya, 14, shares her brother's good looks and quiet, unassuming demeanor. With her dark green eyes, seemingly flawless skin, and oval face framed by

Turn to the next page.

honey-blond hair, you think she is a very pretty girl.

Chatting and enjoying the scenery, you pass through rustic, picturesque farming regions and then begin to ascend a steep slope. Your grandfather navigates the big, old car through one hairpin turn after another as Mrs. Meyers, sitting next to him, studies the road map. Getting a little queasy, you are relieved when the road levels off and you emerge onto a flat plateau. In the near distance, towering mountains loom.

"Start looking for a good picnic spot," says your grandfather, the tires pattering softly and shuddering the car as it passes over railroad tracks.

"How about up there?" asks Shawn, pointing to a grassy spot near the foot of a mountain.

"Looks good to me," says your grandfather, pulling to a stop on a shoulder of the road.

Soon the five of you are digging into your food. And there is a ton of it! You sit in a circle on a blanket. Spread out are long loaves of bread, hunks of cheese, sausage links, fruit, and a variety of soda pop. Everyone eats with a good appetite—too good.

"I'm stuffed!" exclaims Shawn.

"Me, too," you groan, lying down flat on your back.

"Well," suggests your grandfather, "why don't I tell you a little story about this country while your food digests?"

Turn to the next page.

"That's a great idea," Tanya says cheerfully.

"Besides, I don't want to get back in the car on a full stomach. These roads are winding, and I don't want anybody getting sick!" Your grandfather claps his hands and begins to tell his story, his eyes twinkling with mystery.

"As you all probably know, Transylvania is the home of the bloody tales of Count Dracula," he begins with an ominous tone in his voice. "But what you may not know is that the stories are based on the life of a real man, Vlad Tepes. Though perhaps not actually a vampire, Tepes was an incredibly bloodthirsty man, and his nickname, meaning 'son of the devil,' was Dracula."

You laugh. "You're making this up, Grandpa!"

"No," your grandfather says flatly. He adjusts his glasses and gazes at you with a serious look in his eyes. "Vlad Tepes lived during the fifteenth century in a dark and forbidding castle in Transylvania. Much of his time was spent torturing and murdering people. The peasants in the area called him the Impaler, owing to his favorite practice of impaling live victims upon stakes."

"Sick stuff!" exclaims Shawn.

"How horrid!" Tanya gasps, looking green around the gills.

Turn to the next page.

"There is one especially gruesome story about this real-life Prince of Darkness," continues your grandfather. "One day a Turkish envoy came to officially greet the prince Dracula. He ordered them to take off their turbans to show submissiveness. They refused, explaining that it was their custom to keep them on at all times.

" 'Then you shall wear them forever!' screamed Dracula. He had his guards lock the group away. Then he had their turbans nailed to their heads."

"Gross!" Tanya yelps.

"This Vlad Tepes was tough," Shawn observes.

Your grandfather nods.

"And it was based on this man's life that the Dracula stories were written?" you ask in wonder.

"Yes," says your grandfather. "The first of these, of course, was the Irish author Bram Stoker's famous novel, *Dracula*. Stoker had always been intrigued by vampire legends and by stories of the living dead—that is, people turned into zombies by having their blood drained from them. At any rate, there were stories about Vlad Tepes and stories about female vampires as well."

"I think," interrupts Mrs. Meyers gently, "that perhaps this sort of thing is too gory for the kids."

"Aw, Mom," says Shawn, "don't be a spoilsport."

Turn to the next page.

"It's *really* interesting," Tanya says. "I love hearing about this sort of stuff." She smiles at her mother, then puts a hand on your grandfather's sleeve. "Please tell us more."

"Only if your mother agrees," he replies.

Mrs. Meyers shrugs. "Guess I'm outnumbered," she says good-naturedly.

It's a bit chilly, and you pull a blanket over yourself, feeling drowsy from the long drive and the big lunch you've eaten.

"You're not going to fall asleep during my story, are you?" your grandfather asks. "I wouldn't want you to have a nightmare about it."

"No," you assure him. "I'm wide awake."

He smiles as if he knows you are fibbing but continues with his story anyway. "As I was saying, there were stories about female vampires, too. They were also based on the life of a real person, and her name was Elizabeth, the Countess of Nadasy. The countess lived in a castle not far from Transylvania. Like Vlad Tepes, her male counterpart, she enjoyed torturing and murdering people."

"How can anyone *enjoy* that?" you ask in disbelief.

Your grandfather looks embarrassed. "Well, let's just say she had little regard for human life—except her own. In fact, she was obsessed with never getting

Turn to the next page.

old. That's why she had her servants—servants who some say were zombies themselves—kill young people. Completely insane, the countess believed that bathing in their blood would make her young again and give her eternal life. After she had killed more than fifty children, she was found out by the authorities. Her servants were executed, and she was imprisoned in her own castle. Soldiers kept her under constant guard, but still she managed to . . ."

Your grandfather's words are beginning to blur. You want to hear more about the countess, more about Dracula, but you are so drowsy. Your eyelids droop and slowly close. You sleep, but only for a moment. Or is it longer? Five minutes? Thirty? An hour? You sigh and, yawning, open your eyes . . .

And stare in disbelief. Everyone is gone! Day has turned to night, and the moon is a great white disk. Mesmerized, you stare at the bright, white orb. You have never seen a moon like it. This moon, you realize in horror, is dripping with blood!

I must still be asleep, you tell yourself.

"Where is everybody?" you yell into the night.

You hear a rustling behind you. When you turn to see what is there, you nearly faint. Behind you, inches from your face, is a bat with a human head. It bares its fangs, then opens its mouth wider and

Turn to the next page.

wider, so wide that *inside* you can see another world!

Deciding that this *has* to be a dream, you become fascinated and are compelled to explore further. You peer inside the bat's cavernous mouth, now open wide enough for you to step into, and see two people walking in the distance. You run after them. Spellbound, you follow them as they head toward the mouth of a cave.

Finally you catch up to them. It is a boy and a girl. They look back at you, and you are relieved to see Shawn and Tanya.

"Can you believe this wild dream I'm having?" you ask them. "And *you're* in it with me!"

But Shawn and Tanya say nothing. They simply continue walking toward the mouth of the cave. There a form slowly grows . . . into a man . . . into your grandfather! His arms are spread wide, as if he is awaiting you, beckoning you.

"No! Don't go!" a woman screams from somewhere. She runs up to Tanya and Shawn, grasping at them and begging them not to go into the cave. Then she runs to you, and you see it is Shawn and Tanya's mother. "Stop!" she warns the three of you.

But you keep going, following Shawn and Tanya, who still have not spoken. All of you cannot take your eyes off your grandfather as he turns and walks

Turn to the next page.

inside the mouth of the cave, disappearing into the darkness.

Again you hear Mrs. Meyers screaming for you to turn back, but the three of you ignore her.

Rigidly, robotically, you climb lichen-covered stones and boulders and enter the mouth of the cave, which closes behind you with a loud bang. It is as if a huge door made of solid rock has sealed you inside this dark underground world.

Startled, you find yourself staring at Shawn and Tanya. The three of you are inside the cave, and there is no way out. You are surrounded by solid, slimy stone and blackness.

"What happened?" exclaims Shawn, blinking, as though coming out of a trance.

Tanya's eyes slowly open wide. "Where are we?"

"In my nightmare, I think," you reply, gazing about in horror at the dank, suffocating chamber.

The three of you walk around, turning your gaze in every direction and running your hands along the walls. Nowhere is there a crack, an opening, any indication that there is a way out.

But suddenly you realize something. The floor beneath you is moving downward—or is it the walls of the chambers that are moving upward? There is no way to know, no way to find out, and there is

Turn to the next page.

nothing you can do except wait as this macabre change takes place in the cave.

"Look!" shouts Tanya, pointing as a tunnel comes into view ahead.

"Where does it lead?" asks Shawn nervously as the movement of the chamber stops.

You look into the entrance of a tunnel. There is a light flickering eerily at the end. "Only one way to find out," you say. "Follow me."

The three of you walk cautiously down the tunnel. You come to the end of it and find a skeleton holding a torch. Slowly it extends the torch to you. Awestruck, you take it, and as you do the skeleton's finger bones snap off, then the wrist joint, and in a chain reaction, all of it comes apart, collapsing into a dusty pile of bones at your feet.

Shawn screams. Tanya's mouth opens in mute horror. And you stumble backward, torch in hand. You turn to run back down the tunnel, but find yourself staring at a stairwell. One stairway leads up, the other leads down.

"Which way do we go?" asks Shawn, his voice shaking. "It's your dream."

If you head down,
*turn to the **next page**.*

If you head up,
*turn to **page 78**.*

You head down the stairs with your friends close behind, your collective footsteps clattering hollowly on the stairwell.

Ahead you hear a rhythmic squeaking noise followed by a swishing sound. Continuing down, you find that the stairs pass a vast chamber to your right. In this chamber is a pretty, young girl on the biggest, highest swing you have ever seen. The girl is a blond and wears a party dress. Rhythmically she swings back and forth, sucking on a lollipop.

"How strange," whispers Tanya. "Boy, are you having a weird dream!"

The area below the girl on the swing is like a living room, complete with ornate sofas; large, flower-print rugs; and a dining table and four chairs.

"I see you," says the girl, continuing to swing. "I see you peeking round the corner." She giggles. "Wanna come an' play with me?"

You exchange scared looks with your friends.

"What are you gonna do?" the girl asks, swinging on a swing with ropes so long you can't see what they connect to at the top.

Tanya and Shawn look to you to decide.

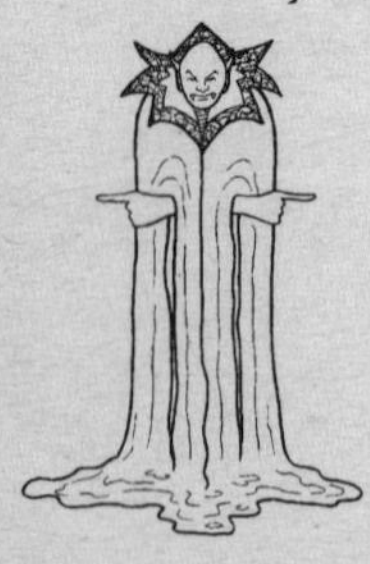

*If you decide to play with the girl, turn to the **next page**.*

*If you keep going down the stairs, **turn to page 24**.*

"That's a pretty cool swing," you tell your friends. "I say we stay and play."

As the three of you enter this part of the cave that looks like a living room, the blond leaps from the swing, rolls into a ball, then straightens and tumbles through the air like an acrobat. Doing flip after flip, she finally lands with a laugh on her feet in front of you.

"Hi! I'm Liz!" she says, her mouth all smeared with bright red lipstick.

As you tell her your names, you notice that the girl is nowhere near as young as you thought. In fact, she is a grown woman about thirty years old who only acts, dresses, and talks as though she were a kid.

"I knew you'd come," she says, running long, red-painted fingernails gently across her cheek.

"What kind of place is this?" you ask, looking around at all the fancy furniture . . . in a cave!

"Don't you like where I live?" she asks coyly.

"It's nice," Shawn says nervously.

"Yeah, it must be cool living in a cave," adds Tanya. "I guess you—"

Stopping Tanya from going on, Liz raises her hand and snaps her fingers. "Servants!" she calls, her voice an echoing bellow that bounces off the stone walls. As the echoing word fades away, three servants emerge out of the darkness carrying large, flickering

Turn to the next page.

candelabra in front of them. They wear red wigs, red velveteen outfits, and red buckled shoes, and behind them come four more servants, dressed identically. They are carrying a large, old-fashioned bathtub with clawed feet.

"I thought you wanted to play," says Shawn.

"Well, silly, obviously I've decided to take a bath instead!"

"She's nuts," you whisper to Shawn and Tanya, as the strange young woman briefly turns her attention to directing the servants where to place the bathtub. "Let's get out of here!"

The three of you turn to flee, only to stand rooted in place, staring in disbelief at dozens of medieval soldiers standing guard behind you. They are in a semicircle blocking the stairwell.

"Where did they come from?" you say with a gasp.

"They don't look very friendly," Tanya observes, backing away, her voice a fear-laced whisper.

"These are my trusty soldiers," snickers the woman. "They are here to serve my every need and obey my every command."

"And who are *you*?" Shawn timidly asks the childlike woman.

Tittering, she puts a lace handkerchief to her lipstick-smeared mouth. Instead of answering, she

Turn to the next page.

flutters her eyelashes and asks, "How old do you think I am?"

"I don't know," you answer.

"Come on, take a wild guess!"

Knowing that sometimes people are sensitive about their age, you make a guess on the low side: "Oh, I'd say about twenty-five."

"Uh-uh," she says, shaking her head. "You're *way* off!" She smiles at Shawn. "How old would you guess I am, Mr. Muscle Man?"

"I really don't know, ma'am," says Shawn, his eyes nervously flitting from the woman to the guards.

"Take a guess!"

"About twenty-one, ma'am," he says with a shrug.

"You're even further off!" she exclaims. "You're off by over two hundred years. I'm three hundred and nine years old! Isn't that something? Isn't that the most marvelous thing you've ever heard?"

"Who . . . who *are* you?" you ask again, petrified to hear the answer.

She curtsies in her puffy, pink chiffon dress. "I am Liz—Elizabeth, actually," she says, waggling ring-laden fingers. "Elizabeth, the Countess of Nadasy."

"No!" you cry as the strong arms of soldiers grab hold of you, Tanya, and Shawn. "You're the woman who—"

Turn to the next page.

"Who what, my child?"

"The woman my grandfather told me about. The Countess of Nadasy, who lived hundreds of years ago in Transylvania."

"And what else did your grandfather tell you about me?"

"That you were insane!" Shawn blurts out for you.

"Still am," the countess says almost proudly.

"And you murdered people—*young* people!" cries Tanya.

"Still do," she adds, batting her eyelashes.

"And you—you murdered them hoping to stay young yourself," you stammer.

"Still hoping to," she says, and then howls with delight. "Because, as you can see, it works!"

The countess's servants and guards press closer, and the horrid cavern erupts with a chorus of their laughter as several guards grab hold of the three of you.

"Fifteen quarts," the countess says, smiling broadly, revealing red lipstick on her teeth. "Yes, I'd say about fifteen quarts."

"What do you mean?" you cry, watching in horror as four servants hoist the bathtub, carry it closer, and set it down on the carpeting in front of you.

"Give or take an itty bit," says the countess, "the

Turn to the next page.

average person has five quarts of blood. And there's one . . . two . . . three of you. And three times five is fifteen, and fifteen quarts of blood mixed with ten of milk and a pinch of perfume will make for an absolutely lovely bath!"

The servants and soldiers part as a huge man wearing a black hood comes toward you.

"Ah, yes! The blood of the young," declares the countess, smiling grotesquely, "*that*—and that alone—is the secret to eternal life!"

You scream as the hooded man comes toward you, candlelight reflecting a red glow off the blade of the knife in his hand.

"That girl is weird with a capital W!" you tell your friends. "Let's get out of here!"

"Won't get any argument from me," says Shawn.

"Me neither!" adds Tanya.

"Boo-hoo, boo-hoo," cries the girl on the swing as you hurry down the stairs. "You won't come and play today . . . and so I say to you, boo-hoo, I don't like you, anyway!"

You continue down the stairs, leaving the strange girl behind. The stairs seem to go on forever, but finally you reach a landing. Your torches have almost burned out. Before throwing them away, in the last few flickerings of feeble light you see that to the left is a walkway leading off into the dark. Straight ahead is a door with EXIT written above it, and to your right is a tunnel.

If you head left down the walkway,
*turn to the **next page**.*

If you enter the tunnel,
*turn to **page 39**.*

If you exit through the door,
*turn to **page 45**.*

You are not fond of tunnels and the exit sign might be a trick, so you decide to head left down the walkway. The air is rank and stale, and all is pitch black. No matter where you look it is so dark you can't see your hand in front of your face.

Tanya suddenly screams. "There's something here in the dark with us!" she cries. "A *lot* of somethings!"

"They're all around us!" yells Shawn.

Then you feel them, too—thousands of invisible hands touching you! Whirling around, the three of you bump into each other as well as into *other* bodies. Then you hear whispers and feel invisible arms reach out to grab you.

"They're people!" yells Tanya. "Invisible people!"

Shawn is thrashing and slapping at them, and for a moment his bodybuilder's strength and bulk take their toll on the invisible beings. The three of you break free and run in terror.

"Look!" you shout.

Ahead, faintly discernible, the cave branches left and right.

"Which way?" yells Tanya. "Make a decision—NOW!"

If you take the left branch,
turn to the ***next page.***

If you take the right branch,
turn to ***page 30.***

Grabbing Shawn and Tanya's hands, you head left and plunge onward through the blacker-than-night tunnel.

Suddenly you hear the whispering again. It sounds like prayers or pleas for help. Again the hands begin touching you and the arms try to wrap around you, as though to hold you back and keep you in place. The embraces are frantic, almost loving, and filled with need.

"Who—*what* are they?" screams Tanya.

"Get away from us!" yells Shawn, thrashing and slugging at the invisible beings. "Leave us alone!"

You, too, are lashing out, and you manage to knock some of the creatures aside. Finally you and your friends are, at least momentarily, free of them again. You race off into the blackness until all at once a blue light goes on, startling you. It fills the cave, bathing the three of you in bizarre luminescence. The source of the light is undetectable. It seems to be coming from nowhere . . . and from *everywhere* . . . at the same time.

"I feel sick," says Tanya. And she *looks* sick, too. All of you do, with your faces and bodies lit blue.

"It's the light that's doing it," says Shawn. "I don't feel so hot either."

You are about to comment that you also feel

Turn to the next page.

funny, but suddenly the blue light goes off and once more you are sealed up in total blackness. You hear the whispering again, and are seized with new fear. The three of you grip each other's hands as the invisible things begin to poke, prod, and grab at you again.

"Just keep going," you urge your friends. "Pretend they're not there."

You are pushing through a great crowd of the things now . . . a hissing, whispering, all-encompassing invisible mob. And there is something new now. Is it your imagination, or do you hear laughter? Soft, odd, hard-to-hear laughter—that is what *seems* to be all around you.

"Don't pay any attention to it!" you yell. "Just keep going!"

There is more laughter. And as you lunge along in the cave, you feel a stale breeze against your skin. "Maybe we're nearing the way out," you say in a hopeful tone. Holding your friends' hands, you turn a corner. The breeze is suddenly stronger, and it smells fresh . . . and then you see the light! It is the mouth of the cave! Running toward it, you emerge onto a rocky stretch of ground. You gaze upward into a starlit night, then hear your name being called.

"It's my grandfather!" you exclaim, suddenly spotting him.

Turn to the ***next page.***

He—and Mrs. Meyers—come into view, the two of them canvassing the rocky landscape with flashlights in hand, looking for you.

"Grandfather!" you yell. "I'm over here. I'm—" And then you stop yourself, frozen in horror, as you realize the hands you are holding, the hands you thought belonged to your friends . . . are invisible! You can feel them, but no hands, and no *people*, are there.

"Shawn!" you cry. "Tanya!"

But the beings holding your hands do not answer you. Instead they laugh. You pull your hands free from them, only to scream in anguish, only to find that your hands are invisible, too . . . and so are your arms, your legs, and the rest of you!

In horror, you run to your grandfather and, weeping, grab his arm.

"Something just touched me!" he exclaims to Mrs. Meyers.

"What?" she asks. "What touched you?"

"I don't know."

"It's me, Grandfather!" you cry. But your voice is only a tiny, inaudible whisper. In desperation, you throw your arms around him.

He lets out a yell and knocks you away. You stumble and almost fall, but something grabs hold of you and keeps you from hitting the ground. Then there

Turn to the next page.

are more of them, dozens of invisible hands and arms grabbing you, dragging you back into the cave.

"Shawn! Tanya!" you cry, barely able to make out your own voice. "Are you in here?"

Giggling laughs erupt all around you in the dark.

"They tricked me!" you cry. "They've made me just like them!"

"Just like them!" giggles a voice, mimicking you. Then others join in: *"Just like them! Just like them! Just like them!"*

"Shawn! Tanya!" you cry again. "Are you in here?"

"Yes," whispers Shawn.

"Yes," whispers Tanya.

"What do we do?" you beg.

"Stay," whispers Shawn.

"We are one of them now," says Tanya, her voice a faint hiss. "Stay," whisper a thousand voices. "Stay with us . . . forever."

You head right, feeling your way along the dark walls. It seems that for now you have left behind the invisible beings, but you are disgusted when you realize that the walls of the cave are wet and slimy.

And suddenly there are no walls at all. You are walking on what seems to be a soft, slick ribbon over a dark, frightening void. In the blackness, you can make out the outlines of what appear to be thick ropes hanging from the ceiling. You pause for a moment and touch the ropes, which glisten in the dark.

"What is this?" you ask, squeezing the odd fiber.

No one has a clue, and the three of you continue along the spongy, ribbonlike walkway, seeing almost nothing below, and even less ahead. All that you can make out clearly are the ropes dangling about you.

Suddenly the strange walkway you are on begins to move beneath your feet. Briefly it is still. Then the trembling starts anew, and becomes more violent.

"We're going to fall!" yells Shawn. "Grab hold of the ropes and hang on!"

"No! Head back!" says Tanya vehemently.

Their eyes wide with fear, your friends look to you to make the decision.

*If you grab hold of the ropes, turn to the **next page**.*

*If you head back, turn to **page 36**.*

"Let's get off this thing!" you shout as you grab hold of one of the thickest of the glistening white ropes. Wrapping your legs around it, hand over hand, you descend into the void below.

Taking your lead, Shawn and Tanya follow, each on a different strand of rope. Soon they are right alongside you, going lower and lower into the dark void. As the three of you descend, the air becomes humid, so moist and warm you are soon drenched with sweat. Your clothes stick to you and your palms are wet . . . and slippery. You grip the strange rope tighter, fearful of losing your grip altogether and falling into who knows what.

Clouds of vapor waft past you. They become thicker and soon enshroud you. Blinded by the black-gray mist, you are about to panic when suddenly the clouds part and you find yourself descending into a clear, semidark void.

"Shawn, how're you doin'?" you call over to your friend as he comes into view slightly above you.

"Fine," he says, breathing hard. "But I'm scared—and I don't mind admitting it."

"What are all those things?" asks Tanya, pointing at massive, twisted shafts of black-brown wood that crisscross overhead, intertwine below, and jut out at all angles.

Turn to the next page.

Looking over your shoulder and then down, you see Tanya, behind and below you.

"I'm not sure," you answer, "but they look like the branches of a tree—a dead tree."

"But how could there be a tree in a cave?" asks Shawn. "Not to mention the fact that it looks as tall as a ten-story building!"

"Who knows? Maybe it isn't a tree at all," you say. "In this dream it looks like anything can happen!" You continue to descend, your eyes directed below to where the vertical rope you are on intersects with—and connects to—a horizontal rope of the same stuff.

The three of you step onto the bouncy, soft strand. After pausing to catch your breath, you resume your descent, down other vertical strands, which in turn connect with more horizontal strands. The strands are getting thinner, shorter, and closer together, and soon you find yourself in what seems to be a corded crosshatch.

You take another breather by standing on one of the horizontal strands. Looking above and below, you see a huge, gently undulating network of interconnecting white strands—a great huge webwork suspended between the gnarled branches of the huge, dead tree. Suddenly you realize where you are and freeze in terror.

Turn to the next page.

"We're on a spiderweb!" yells Shawn, confirming your fear.

"We've gotta go back!" shrieks Tanya.

You study the web above and below, as well as the tree. "At least I don't see any spiders," you observe.

As you dangle in the monstrous spiderweb, wondering what to do, it begins to rain . . . *inside* the cave.

The first raindrop passes right by you. It is huge, glistening, and misses the spiderweb as well. It hits far below with a monstrous splash. Then more drops fall, and a dark wind begins to blow. The wind causes the web to waver, and the raindrops hitting the strands jar the whole thing, causing it to vibrate like a mass of guitar strings.

Shawn, above you, is yelling out a warning over the now thunderous roar of the rain. But there is no need—you and Tanya already realize your peril and are hanging onto the web for dear life.

Suddenly Shawn lets out a cry—as a giant drop slams into him. Before you know it, he has fallen right on you, causing you to lose your balance and bump Tanya. Toppling off the web, the three of you tumble through space.

With a bounce, you land on your back in the tightly woven center of *another* web. You rise up and down on the gossamer mesh—stuck to it as it undulates.

Turn to the next page.

The sensation is bizarre, as intriguing as it is scary. You feel as though you are glued to a trampoline, bouncing up and down in slow motion.

"I can't move!" screams Tanya.

"I'm stuck!" wails Shawn.

You are helpless too, but try to look on the bright side. "At least the web broke our fall," you tell your friends. "Besides, so far I haven't seen any—"

And then you realize there is no longer truth to the statement you were about to make. Far above you, something is descending from a branch. Rapidly it is getting larger and larger. "No!" you scream as you catch sight of a spider unlike anything you have ever seen before. It has sixteen clawed, furry legs joined to a grotesque body—which isn't a body at all, but rather a pulsing, reddish-brown brain!

For a heart-stopping moment, you think the spider is coming at you. Then you realize it is not—it is plummeting directly toward Shawn!

As the monster lands on your friend, closing its barbed, deadly legs on him, Shawn fights with all his might. But with his arms glued to sticky webbing, about all he can do is howl hysterically.

"Shawn!" cries Tanya, also struggling against the gluey web. And then she looks at you. "We've got to save him!" she screams.

Turn to the next page.

Helpless, you watch as the claws of the thing squeeze Shawn, tightening around him like a vise. Then a transparent, needlelike thing—a fang of some sort—protrudes from the spider's brainlike body, poises for an instant, then plunges straight down into your helpless friend.

"No!" you and Tanya scream in unison.

There is nothing you can do but watch as Shawn's body goes soft, becomes gelatinous, and turns to liquid that is being sucked into the transparent fang.

"It-it's eating him," Tanya stammers as the two of you stare at the most horrible sight of your lives.

The brain—the body—of the thing bloats with its meal. For a long moment it is still. Then it begins to move—slowly at first, then faster—toward you! Tanya is screaming, but her voice is seemingly far away now. You feel paralyzed, unable to move, unable to even utter a sound. Your eyes are fixed, open in horror, as you look up at the hairy legs, the brain, and the fang, as it plunges toward your heart.

"What if the ropes can't support our weight?" you ask. "I agree with Tanya. Let's head back."

The three of you turn and run together, back along the strange, spongy walkway. You are out of breath, panting, when suddenly the walkway quivers again, almost causing you to fall. You slow your pace. You are moving carefully, and then you suddenly freeze in horror.

Ahead in the ugly, shadowy gloom of the cavern, you see the most frightening and grotesque sight of your life. Out of the stone walls of the cave, like some horrid lichen, grow the shoulders and head of a Goliath-sized man. His flesh is pink and sticky looking. His eyes are blue-green and bulging, and his mouth is open as wide as the mouth of a tunnel, revealing row upon row of serrated teeth.

"Noooo!" screams Tanya, her voice echoing all around you.

She is looking ahead at the man's eyes and then down at his gigantic mouth. She is seeing what you are seeing, realizing what you are realizing: Out of the mouth protrudes an insanely long tongue—and it is on this tongue you have been running!

Shawn sees it, too. "What do we do?!" he screams.

There is no time to answer. You are trying desperately to grab hold of one of the ropelike things

Turn to the next page.

hanging down, but none are close enough to reach. In a blind panic to get off the tongue, Tanya leaps out after a rope, but it is impossibly far away. In horror, you see her hands grab hold of nothing but air. Flailing wildly, she shrieks and falls into the dark, seemingly bottomless void below.

"Tanya!" cries Shawn. "My sister! My sister!"

There is an awful thud far below.

Shawn is kneeling on the edge of the tongue, sobbing over the fate of his sister, but you see that the two of you are in for an equally horrible fate.

Like a long, red carpet being rolled up, the tongue you are on is curling back upon itself, and a massive, ever-growing coil is steamrolling toward you. There is no time to jump, for in seconds the spongy tongue is crushing you in its soft, fleshy folds. As it spirals you around and around, about to deposit you into the humongous mouth, you look up to see the rows of teeth slowly closing down on you. Then all goes black, and though you feel no pain, you hear a loud crunching noise . . . and open your eyes to find yourself at the picnic site!

Rolled up uncomfortably in a blanket, you are listening to your grandfather telling one of his stories. Shawn, sitting next to you, is chomping noisily on a cracker.

Turn to the next page.

"Close your mouth when you eat!" admonishes Tanya.

"Don't you like 'see' food?" Shawn asks, laughing as he sticks out his tongue covered with cracker crumbs and cracker sludge.

"Oh, grow up!" says Tanya.

As Shawn rolls his tongue back into his mouth, you shake your head and try to stay awake. You sure don't want to slip into *that* nightmare again!

You head right, into the dark tunnel. The tunnel intersects with others, and you and your friends grope down one long shaft after another, feeling your way along the dank, gritty walls of stone. The air is stale and rank, but gradually you feel a bit of fresh air, and then a steady breeze. Ahead you see faint light and hurrying along, you find yourselves emerging from the tunnel out onto a road. In the near distance is the dark silhouette of a small town.

"Where are we?" asks Tanya.

"I have no idea," you say, as the three of you trudge along down the road.

Ahead you see streetlights, none of which are on, and soon you find yourselves entering the town. All is dark and quiet.

"This is really bizarre!" exclaims Shawn. "A town *inside* a tunnel!"

You pass a row of houses, then a police station, train station, library, and school. But all of the buildings look fake. Ahead you spot a man.

"Hey, mister!" you yell, running toward him. But you stop in your tracks as you get closer, and stare in puzzlement. The man is not moving. He has a simple, artificial expression on his face.

Touching him, you find he is made of plastic.

Tanya and Shawn also come and inspect the man.

Turn to the next page.

"He looks like some kind of doll," observes Shawn.

Tanya has headed across the street toward a park. You and Shawn follow her, walking across artificial grass past toylike trees.

"I don't get it," Tanya says as you approach. She is staring at a woman with a cocker spaniel on a leash. They, like the man, are made of plastic.

"What *is* this place?" you ask in awe.

"Let's keep exploring," suggests Shawn.

Gravel crunches underfoot as the three of you walk on through the town. You come upon a train stopped on the tracks. In silent silhouette the locomotive sits in front of a coal car, several boxcars, a flatcar, and a caboose. The train is made of real metal—you can feel this by touching it—but something about it is not quite right.

You and Shawn follow Tanya up onto a wooden platform. A man carrying a suitcase is standing there looking at his watch, and standing by the railroad station is a porter. Both men are made of plastic.

"Well," you say to Shawn and Tanya, "I don't know where we are or how we got here, but somehow we need to find a way out."

"Should we hop on the train?" asks Shawn.

You shake your head. "No way. The engineer is probably made of plastic, too. I say we move on."

Turn to the next page.

You jump down from the platform. Your two friends follow suit, and together the three of you head across a field of fake grass.

In the distance looms a purple and white, painted-looking mountain. You step up onto railroad tracks and walk along on them. Ahead the tracks disappear into a tunnel in a mountain.

"This tunnel is made of plastic foam or something," you say as you take a step inside and touch the side of the tunnel. "It feels as if it's—"

Startling you, you hear a tremendous thudding sound, like the footfalls of a giant, and almost in the same instant you are blinded by a flood of light. Hiding just inside the entrance to the tunnel and shielding your eyes from the powerful light, the three of you peer around a corner into a boy's bedroom.

Astonished, you find yourself looking at huge wall posters, gigantic model airplanes, an enormous desk littered with papers, a warehouse-sized closet overflowing with junk, and a tremendous bed with a colossal football helmet hanging by its chin strap from the bedpost. And there's the boy himself—in a T-shirt and jeans and low-cut boots—looking as though he's a hundred feet tall.

For a moment the boy's giant head is haloed by light from a ceiling fixture, and then he sits down on

Turn to the next page.

the floor. In front of him is the control box of a train set, with switching mechanisms and wires connected to tracks that circle and crisscross around his room.

"All aboard!" he yells, his voice exploding in your ears.

As you cower in the entrance of the tunnel, you watch as his huge finger pushes a button on a remote control. Suddenly you hear metal wheels turn on the metal track. A train whistle screeches, and in horror you realize what is going on. In the distance of this oversized room, you see the railroad station you just saw . . . and although the plastic people aren't moving, the train is! Quickly it gathers speed and soon is rattling around the track, going faster and faster toward the tunnel where you, Tanya, and Shawn are crouching. It crosses a meadow of artificial grass, disappears from view behind a mountain, then slows as it crosses a bridge over a fake river.

"We're in a kid's room," whispers Tanya. "One with a train set in it."

"Only we're tiny," cries Shawn. "And everything else is huge!"

Again the train whistle screams, nearly breaking your eardrums.

As you backpedal into the tunnel, then turn and run, the three of you feel the track vibrating beneath

Turn to the next page.

your feet. A deafening mechanical roar and light fills the tunnel. Looking over your shoulder as you run, you see the single headlight of the locomotive, and directly ahead is the end of the tunnel.

Panic drives you through the tunnel opening, and you jump aside, just as the train roars past. . . . But Shawn and Tanya are not as lucky. You hear their terrified screams as the huge wheels roll over them, spattering you with blood.

In a state of shock, paralyzed with horror, you lie beside the track, the blood of your friends dripping off you. You feel sickened, and tears of anguish course down your cheeks as the train rumbles away.

A huge face, that of the boy, comes closer and an eye larger than your body studies you. His vast gap of a mouth moves. "Are you all right?" he asks, his voice a thunderous blast in your ear.

You roll away, sobbing, hardly caring now if the boy-giant chooses to squash you like a fly.

The question is repeated: "Are you all right?"

A hand shakes your shoulder.

You open your eyes . . . and sit up on the picnic blanket, bathed in sweat, your body shaking.

Your grandfather is looking worriedly at you. "Are you all right?" he asks. "You were crying in your sleep."

Turn to the next page.

"Were you having a nightmare?" asks Mrs. Meyers.

"An awful one," you say, as bits and pieces of your dream come flashing back into your mind. You look around. "Where are Shawn and Tanya?" you ask.

"They went for a walk," says Mrs. Meyers, pointing off in the general direction of a bridge over a stream that leads directly into a tunnel in a mountain. "They're following the old tracks through—"

Already you are running as fast as you can down the slope and out onto the bridge. "Shawn! Tanya!" you yell as you burst into the tunnel. Ahead you spot two silhouettes. "Tanya! Shawn!" you scream. "Get out of this tunnel! There's a train about to—"

"No there isn't," calls Shawn lightheartedly.

"But there will be!" you yell as you catch up to them. "I know, because—"

A shrill whistle sounds somewhere behind you, and looking over your shoulder you see the headlight of a locomotive entering the tunnel. Grabbing Tanya and Shawn, you jump aside, out of harm's way, as the train thunders by.

"Let's take the exit!" you exclaim. "It's time to exit outta here!"

Tanya and Shawn nod in vigorous agreement. You push open the door, and the three of you find yourselves stepping out onto rolling vistas of open farmland.

"Where are we?" asks Shawn, his eyes filled with wonder.

"This doesn't look at all like where we were when we went into the cave," says Tanya. "I don't see my mom or your grandfather anywhere."

Together, feeling a bit apprehensive and confused, you and your friends cross a meadow and then head up along a dusty, winding road. Ahead in the distance you spot an old, dilapidated house.

"Look at that weird place!" you exclaim to your friends, pointing. "Let's go check it out."

"Might as well," says Tanya.

The three of you head toward the old house. Coming around a bend in the path, you happen upon an old man. He is hunched over and wears a dirty, badly stained overcoat.

"Mornin'," he says as the words whistle out of a mouth of rotted teeth, many of which are missing. "Where're you headed?"

"Well," says Shawn, "for right now, to check out

Turn to the next page.

that old place up ahead."

"Wouldn't if I was you," warns the old man, running his fingers through his long, gray hair. "Place is haunted. Terrible things happened there a long time ago. *Terrible* things."

"Like what?" Shawn asks.

"Best you don't know, sonny. Just don't go there. Mark my words!" Shaking his head, wrapping his coat tighter about himself, the old man heads down the road. He gives you an odd look over his shoulder, then continues on his way.

"You two still want to go?" asks Tanya, a nervous edge to her voice.

"Sure," you say. "Why not? If you ask me, that man was just wacko."

"You sure?" asks Shawn.

You nod your head firmly. "There's no such thing as ghosts," you say with conviction. "So there's no way that house is haunted. Let's go."

The three of you head off in the direction of the house. But as you approach the place, it *does* give you the creeps. The walls, once painted red, look as though they have a skin disease. Red flakes and scabs of paint are peeling off all over the place. The roof is in no better shape as it sags in the middle, and its shingles are weathered, twisted, and warped, bent

Turn to the next page.

back by wind, sun, and rain.

"Let's get out of here," says Shawn. "This place really bothers me."

"Oh, don't be such a chicken," says Tanya with a soft laugh.

Though the remark is just a teasing one, Shawn looks hurt.

"I'm no chicken," he says, puffing up his chest. "It's just that there're things I'd rather do than hang around this disgusting old place." Though he tries to hide it, there is still genuine fear in Shawn's eyes.

Tanya looks knowingly from her brother to you. "We both know he's chicken. What do you want to do?" she asks.

If you want to check out the house,
turn to the ***next page.***

If you want to leave the house,
turn to ***page 55.***

"Come on," you say, stepping up onto the rickety porch. You pull open a ripped screen door then knock on a wooden door that creaks open at your touch.

"Well, hello there," says the gray outline of a seated female form, her voice only a hoarse croak. "Please come in."

Nervous and wary, you stare into the gloom and see a white-haired elderly woman sitting in a wooden chair by a softly glowing fire. Though her clothes are old-fashioned and dowdy, and her hair is pulled back in a tight bun, the woman has a pleasant, friendly face. A cute, black-and-brown tabby cat springs onto the table, looking at the three of you with cockeyed whiskers twitching. Then in one fluid motion, it steps down into its mistress's lap and curls into a ball.

"I'm Celia Crane," says the woman. "And you are . . . ?"

You introduce yourself and your friends and begin to relax as you look around the place. The house is old and small, but it is clean, warm, and nicely furnished.

Celia Crane smiles gently. "Forgive me for saying so," she says, "but you seem a little nervous. Why?"

"Is this place haunted?" blurts Shawn.

"You idiot, Shawn!" says Tanya, frowning, as she

Turn to the next page.

pokes him in the side.

Celia Crane laughs. "My dear, no! My house may be old, but it surely is not haunted."

"See!" you say, rolling your eyes at Shawn.

"Sorry," he says a bit sheepishly. "I didn't mean to be rude."

"That's quite all right, young man," says Celia Crane, stroking the tabby in her lap, which is purring contentedly, its eyes half closed.

"It's just that we met this old man, and he said that—" Shawn begins defensively, but he is cut off by Tanya, who hisses at him to be quiet.

"Would you youngsters care for a bite to eat?" Celia asks, gesturing in the direction of a small kitchen. "I could make you a sandwich or offer you some milk and shortbread."

"No, that's all right," you say. "We have to be on our way. But thank you very much."

"I understand," she says, a slight note of disappointment in her voice.

Realizing the woman is probably very lonely and craves company, you feel guilty for not staying, but Tanya and Shawn are already headed for the door. And Celia Crane, carrying her cat, is following you.

"Well, have a nice day, dears," she says in her raspy voice. Smiling, she takes her cat's paw between

Turn to the next page.

thumb and index finger and waves bye-bye with it, then disappears behind the closing door.

"See, that old man *was* wacky," says Tanya, as the three of you head down the porch steps. "He and his stories about that house being hau—"

She stops herself abruptly, midword. From inside the house comes a thump and a bang—like a chair falling over. The squall of a cat mixes with a rhythmic creaking noise.

"Wh-what was that?" stammers Shawn.

"I don't know," you say, heading back toward the house. "It sounded as though—"

"I told you not to go there!" bellows a voice behind you.

Already standing before the door, the three of you turn as one, and behind you is the old man in the heavy coat. His dark, glassy eyes narrow into beads of suspicion. "What're you doing here? I told you not to come here!"

"We felt like it," says Shawn defiantly.

"Calm down," says Tanya, putting a hand on her brother's shoulder.

"Hey, mister," you ask. "How come you said this house is haunted?"

"You went in there?" he asks, raising an eyebrow.

"Yes," answers Tanya, "and there sure weren't any

Turn to the next page.

ghosts to speak of."

"Just a nice, elderly lady," you add. "She even offered us a snack."

The man laughs, guffawing until he coughs. He shakes his head, laughs again. "Her name didn't happen to be Celia, Celia Crane, did it?"

"Yes," you answer. "You know her?"

"I did."

"Did?"

"Oh, yeah . . . when she was alive," the man says, chuckling. "She died about eight months ago."

Puzzled, a bit scared, you turn back to the house. "But she can't be dead. We just talked to her." You turn back toward the door and knock on it loudly. This time it doesn't open on its own, nor does anyone answer. You knock again, louder.

"I tell you, she's dead," says the old man with a mocking sneer.

You try the doorknob and it turns easily in your hand. You push open the door, and with Tanya and Shawn on your heels, you enter the place . . . and stare in horror and disbelief.

"She keeps comin' back to do it, over an' over," says the man, laughing as he follows the three of you inside.

The once tidy, clean house is now foul and dirty. A patina of dust covers everything, and draperies of

Turn to the ***next page.***

cobwebs enshroud the place. From a rafter hangs the corpse of Celia Crane, one rotted hand grasping the rope from which her body hangs. Flies buzz all around her eyes, which are nothing but empty sockets. Below her on the floor is one shoe and an overturned wooden chair.

"Hung herself . . . again!" the old man exclaims.

"But we just talked to her!" Tanya cries.

"Wasn't *her* you was talkin' to," corrects the old man. " 'Twas her ghost." He points at the corpse, then puts his hand right through it. "Even this ain't her. You see, old Celia, she likes to keep hangin' herself. Likes the attention, you know." He turns to the ghostly body. "Like to keep scarin' people . . . don't you, Celia?"

"Yes," answers the corpse in a raspy voice. She closes her shriveled eyelids over empty sockets as the tabby leaps onto the overturned chair. She suddenly reopens the lids to reveal the vibrant, healthy eyes of a younger person. She blinks. "Like what you see?" Celia asks.

Horrified, nauseated, you stare.

"Let's get out of here!" Shawn screams. But he remains rooted to the spot, as though his feet were nailed to the floor.

"I'm so pretty, oh so pretty . . ." sings the corpse.

Turn to the next page.

"Quiet, Celia dear," scolds the old man.

Her mouth freezes open.

"That's better, dear," he laughs.

"Wh-who are *you*?" Shawn demands of the old man.

"Nicholas Crane," he replies.

"Crane?" You look at the corpse, then at the man. "Then you must be her . . ."

"Yes," says the corpse, her mouth back to life again, "Nicholas is my husband."

"Hush!" hisses the man through his broken and decayed teeth.

"Did—did you kill her?" stammers Tanya.

"No, Celia killed herself, like I told you." The old man angrily pushes the corpse, causing it to swing back and forth on the rope. He looks with contempt at the swinging body. "Why aren't you in your grave?" he demands.

"So I could come back and kill myself again," she answers with a wormy giggle. "So I could torture *you*!"

"Well, get back in your grave!" orders Nicholas Crane.

The body continues to swing, like a pendulum . . . and each time it goes back and forth it gets fainter, as though being erased. "Goodbye," it intones. "For now." And then it is gone.

Turn to the next page.

"Hideous thing!" mutters Nicholas Crane, shaking his gray head.

You don't know what to do or say. You open your mouth to speak, but no words come out.

"Wh-why did she do it?" stammers Shawn, his usually strong voice reduced to a timid whisper. "You said your wife killed herself. Why?"

"Guilt," answers the old man matter-of-factly.

"Guilt over what?"

Crane's eyes open wide. "Murder!" he snarls.

"She *murdered* somebody?" you ask.

"Yes!" he exclaims, growing agitated.

You are afraid to ask the next question, afraid you already know the answer. "Who—who did she murder?" you manage to get out.

"Me," he says, laughing evilly as he recedes, fades, and disappears, leaving the three of you standing alone in the middle of the dusty, broken-down little house, wondering what is real and what is not . . . but worst of all wondering if you will ever get out of this nightmare.

You realize that Shawn really would prefer not going into the house, and it's not going to make much difference to you or Tanya one way or the other.

"Nah," you say, "let's keep going. We've got more important things to do than snoop around in some old house. For one thing, we need to find your mom and my grandfather."

The three of you continue along the road. The landscape is a vast, rolling green meadow, the monotony interrupted here and there by gargantuan, sun-baked boulders and large, gnarled oak trees.

"Hi," a squeaky little voice pipes up.

Startled, you look around, then up, and see a young boy looking down at you from a tree house. He leaps into space, and at the last second grabs hold of a heavy rope and swings out into the air Tarzan-style. Then he drops to the ground in front of you. "Hi," he says again. "I'm Roger."

You introduce yourself and your friends, studying the boy as you do. Skinny and freckle-faced, he is dressed in an old plaid shirt, blue jeans with the knees worn out, and high-top sneakers.

"Want to play a game?" he asks.

"Well," you say, "actually, we're looking for some people. Maybe you've seen them."

You describe your grandfather and Mrs. Meyers.

Turn to the next page.

"Have you seen them?"

"No, but maybe Mr. Gibbs has," the boy replies.

"Who's Mr. Gibbs?" asks Tanya.

"I'll take you to him," offers Roger.

"But who *is* he?" you ask again.

"Mr. Gibbs is real rich, and he lives alone in a big house," the boy answers. "He's sort of bored, if you want to know the truth. Most of the time he just plays solitaire. But he loves to have visitors. He likes to do magic tricks for his visitors, and most of all he likes to play games, all sorts of *special* games."

"What kind of *special* games?" you ask with genuine curiosity.

"They're hard to explain," says Roger. "Hard for *me* to explain, but not for Mr. Gibbs."

"Well," says Shawn, "I'm not so much interested in his hobbies and games, but if he can tell us where my mom and—"

"Can't promise anything," Roger interrupts. "All I can do is take you to meet him. *You* can ask him anything you want." Roger shrugs. "So do you want to meet him?"

*If you go with Roger to meet Mr. Gibbs, turn to the **next page**.*

*If you don't go with him, turn to **page 67**.*

Hoping Mr. Gibbs will be able to lead you back to your grandfather and Mrs. Meyers, you and your friends head off with Roger. Soon you find yourselves approaching a large, sprawling house. Roger knocks, and calls out hello, entering without waiting for a reply. The three of you follow him through the modernistic, split-level interior of the house. Footsteps clicking hollowly on highly polished parquet wooden floors, you enter a huge, semicircular room overlooking the surrounding countryside. Standing at one of the picture windows with his back to you is a man in a business suit, gazing out at the rolling fields. At your approach, he slowly turns around.

"Welcome," says the tall, impeccably dressed dark-haired man, his tone gentle and friendly.

You are about to speak when he reaches behind your ear and pulls out a silver coin. He tosses it to you, and you laugh as he does the same thing to Tanya and Shawn. Then he reaches inside his jacket pocket . . . and takes out *your* watch.

"How'd you do that?" you ask, looking at your bare wrist. Your watch had been there just a moment ago.

The man shrugs. "Just a simple little trick."

"Do another one, Mr. Gibbs!" Roger says excitedly.

"Yeah!" exclaims Shawn.

Mr. Gibbs looks at him. "How about a card trick,

Turn to the next page.

young man?" he asks Shawn, seeming to pluck a deck of cards out of the air. He shuffles them in a way that looks like he's opening and closing an accordion. "Oh, dear," he says, as he continues to shuffle. "We have a problem. This deck has only 51 cards in it! Young man—would you kindly give me the jack of hearts?"

"But I don't have it," says Shawn, looking puzzled.

"Now, don't kid around," says Mr. Gibbs, smiling. "You know it's under your shoe—your *left* one, to be exact."

"Huh?" says Shawn, picking up his foot. Then with surprise written all over his face, he picks up a card that is lying there. It is the jack of hearts.

"*That* is amazing!" exclaims Tanya. "How'd you do that?"

"The same way I did this," says Mr. Gibbs. Snapping the fingers of his left hand, he produces a pouchlike leather bag in his right hand. Opening it, he spreads out its contents—shimmering gold nuggets!

"Is it real?" you ask, touching the gold.

He nods. "Would you like it—*all* of it?"

"Sure," you say, "but, I mean, can I just *have* it?"

"Sort of," pipes Roger.

"What do you mean?" you ask, growing a little nervous.

Turn to the next page.

"What he means," says Mr. Gibbs, "is a prize such as this has to be won—by playing a game."

"The game's called Treasure Hunt," says Roger excitedly, seeming near bursting with anticipation. "You'll love it! And it's guaranteed—you *always* end up with the gold!"

"How do you play?" you ask Mr. Gibbs.

"You are given the bag of gold, and it is your goal to hide with it in the woods. Your friends are given a map. It is their goal to go find you. If they find you within ten minutes, which is all the time they'll be given, you split the gold three ways. If they don't find you within this period, you get *all* the gold." His dark eyes study you. "Would you like to play?" he asks with a wide smile.

If you wish to play,
turn to the ***next page.***

If you decide not to play,
turn to ***page 64.***

"Sure," you say, "I'll play. What do I have to lose?"

"Oh boy!" exclaims Roger.

"Now what you have to do," says Mr. Gibbs, "is this." He reaches into the breast pocket of his suit and takes out a folded sheet of pink paper and hands it to you. "Study that for a moment."

Unfolding the pink paper you see that it is a map. The route you are to take has been clearly marked.

"Now put the map in this," says Mr. Gibbs, handing you a pink envelope, "and give it to your friends."

You do as you are told, handing the envelope to Shawn. Mr. Gibbs instructs him to put it in his pocket, which he does.

"Now what?" you ask eagerly.

Mr. Gibbs scoops up the gold, refills the pouch, and looks at his watch. "You will now go to your hiding place with Roger. Your friends will be given ten minutes to find you." He smiles, a dark gleam in his eyes. "Do you want them to find you?" he asks, handing you the bag of gold.

"Well, no," you say. "If they find me, I don't get to keep all of the gold."

"Exactly what I thought you'd say," says Mr. Gibbs, clapping his hands with delight.

Roger giggles.

Mr. Gibbs's eyes open wide, and his once mellow

Turn to the next page.

voice is a booming explosion. "Now go to your destination!" he orders.

Suddenly everything spins, and you find yourself in the middle of an inward-winding circle. Then everything goes dark and you hear Roger laugh. Looking up toward a source of light, you see him standing in a field on the lip of an open grave . . . in which you lie.

"You've reached your destination!" Roger yells down at you. "Your *final* destination . . . unless your friends find you."

You stare around you in abject horror at white satin, and then you realize where you are—in a coffin at the bottom of a freshly dug grave! There is a small, rectangular glass window at eye level in the lid, and above your mouth there is a circle of perforated openings, like those of a speaker. Rolling your eyes back, you can see a penlight-sized lightbulb, which gives off a feeble glow. You are cramped and can barely move your body in any direction. In your hands is the bag of gold.

"*Now* do you want your friends to find you?" laughs Roger, leaning on a shovel high above you.

"Yes!" you sob. "Yes, yes I do!"

Roger scoops up a shovelful of soil from a mound of dirt. "I'll *bet* you do," he says, flinging soil into the

Turn to the next page.

grave, which lands with clattering drumbeats on the lid. Repeatedly he drives the shovel into the mound and tosses thundering shovelfuls of rock and dirt onto the coffin.

"Why are you doing this?" you cry.

Roger pauses for a moment and looks down at you. "'Cause Mr. Gibbs and I like it."

"Let me out!" you plead.

Roger shrugs. "Can't do that," he says simply. "Your only hope is that your friends find you."

"How much time has elapsed?" you beg. "Have they started looking yet?"

"Not until I return from your—" he giggles. "Your hiding place. Not until then can they open the envelope, take out the map, and start looking. The map's easy enough to follow, but there is one tricky thing about it."

"What's that?" you ask, stifling a sob.

"The map may not be where you think it is."

"Where is it?" you cry, as earth again begins to rain down on the coffin. You break out in a cold sweat and find it is getting harder and harder to breathe. Panic grips you, and you start to thrash about. Futilely you push up on the lid . . . as fine soil sifts through the speaker. "Where is the map?" you scream, coughing . . . as a shovelful of dirt hits the

Turn to the next page.

window above your eyes, partly obscuring your view. "Where—" you start again . . . as your hand brushes something. From your breast pocket you pull out an envelope. Sobbing, you open it, already knowing what you will find. With trembling hands, screaming hysterically, you unfold the map, which shows a clearly marked route—right to where you are buried.

You are tempted to say yes, that you want to play the game, but for a moment you pause to think. Why would Mr. Gibbs just give away the gold? you ask yourself. There must be some kind of trick.

"No, thank you," you tell him, "but we have to find my grandfather and my friends' mother."

"Oh, come on," groans Tanya. "The game sounds like so much fun."

"Maybe," you say, "but you're forgetting one thing. We're lost in my dream, remember? The most important thing is to find our way out."

"You're right," says Shawn.

"A wise choice," says Roger, suddenly on your side.

"Be quiet, Roger!" snarls Mr. Gibbs.

"You see," says Roger, ignoring the man, "if you'd played his game, you would have ended up like me—*dead*." Reaching up, he grabs hold of his forehead and pulls the flesh down, as though it were a living mask, to reveal a skull. "This is how his little game ends," says the fleshless face that was once Roger. "*Murder* is how it ends."

"Shut up, you little monster!" screams Mr. Gibbs.

You and your friends are terrified; and, backing away from the skeleton of Roger and the horrible Mr. Gibbs, you wonder why they seem to be letting you go. Actually what's left of Roger appears to be taking

Turn to the next page.

sides with you, but if Gibbs is so dangerous, why is he just standing there? His face is red with rage, and though it seems as if he wants to come after you—even kill you—it also seems he can't move and is rooted to the spot.

"Don't you see?" Roger's eyes roll in withered sockets. "He uses me to lure kids here, dazzles them with magic, and then invites them all to play his deadly game."

"He kills kids?" says Tanya, her voice a whisper.

"Lots of 'em. That's his game. And there's only *one* way to win." Roger taps his skull with a skeletal finger. "You have to do what I *didn't* do. You have to use your head. You have to realize that there are games in life you can win only by *never* playing."

"Why isn't he moving?" you ask, pointing at a frozen Mr. Gibbs.

"It's part of the way the game works." Roger breaks into a bony grin. "You have to make a *wrong* move for him to move at all." Roger taps his skull again. "Now think—right this second—what is the best move you can make?"

"I'm outta here!" you yell.

"Me, too!" exclaims Shawn.

"Ditto!" shouts Tanya.

The three of you run from the house. Hurrying

Turn to the next page.

out into bright sunshine, you clamp your eyes closed against the glare . . . and suddenly your feet go out from under you. You land on your back, and startled, you open your eyes . . . to find yourself on your back, lying on the picnic blanket!

As your mind slowly clears, you hear your grandfather talking and turn your head toward him. He is giving one of his lectures, one you've heard many times before. It's the one about how hundreds of kids get hurt and killed each year because they make the stupid mistake of trusting strangers.

You think about how you've always been warned about "interacting with strangers," and decide that in a dream that goes double. "No," you tell Roger. "Thanks anyway, but I think we had better be on our way."

"Suit yourself," he says.

The three of you head off down the road through a copse of trees and then down a short slope. Suddenly you find the dirt road you are on intersecting with a paved highway, and coming up the highway is the car your grandfather rented!

He pulls up beside you and rolls down the window. "Where've you been?" he asks, sitting in the front passenger seat.

"We've been looking all over for you," says Mrs. Meyers, from behind the wheel.

The three of you clamber into the backseat, and Mrs. Meyers puts the car into gear. "We've been frantic with worry," she says as the car gathers speed. "We went for a walk, and when we came back to the picnic site, you were gone. Where on earth did you go?"

"We're not sure," you say. "We went into a cave. Only maybe we didn't go into a cave. I may have just been dreaming. In fact, maybe *this* is just a dream."

Your grandfather looks puzzled, and you are about to explain when a few raindrops hit the windshield.

Turn to the next page.

Only they are not rain. They are red drops of blood. Mrs. Meyers shrieks and hits the brakes. As she does the car begins to skid on the blood-covered highway, but she manages to straighten it out.

Struggling to keep a level head, she turns her attention to the unfamiliar panel above the gearshift and manages to turn on the windshield wipers. But instead of clearing the windshield, the wipers leave twin opaque red smears on the glass. The road ahead is now a crimson-tinted blur.

"Look at the sky!" Shawn exclaims.

You look up through your window and see that the sky is bloated with black-purple clouds from which veinlike tendrils hang.

"What do I do?" Mrs. Meyers begs.

"Stop the car!" yells Tanya.

"Don't! Don't try to stop again!" says your grandfather. "You'll just go into another skid."

"Keep going!" yells Shawn. "You've got to get out of here!"

You are the only one who has yet to voice an opinion . . .

If you tell Mrs. Meyers to keep going,
*turn to the **next page**.*

If you tell her to stop,
*turn to **page 74**.*

"Keep going, Mrs. Meyers," you say as calmly as you can.

She glances over her shoulder at you, and you can see that she still has her doubts. Nevertheless, she does as you say.

The highway ahead is puddled with red, and rivulets of blood are swirling along the shoulders of the road. Out the blotchy side windows, you see great draperies of bloody rain coloring the countryside a gory scarlet. Hills, trees, fields, and even farmhouses—all are now drenched in red.

Everyone is horrified, but Tanya seems to be the worst off. Her eyes look glued open and her mouth moves continuously, forming words only she can hear.

Suddenly great bolts of lightning begin to smack the earth. Thunder rumbles and rattles the car windows, and to this awful music, great zigzagging, electrical spiders of lightning dance together in grotesque and mindless patterns across the sky.

Even with the windows of the car closed, you become aware of the stench of blood that has literally been "fried" by lightning. With each bolt, the odor becomes stronger and more nauseating.

Finally it starts to rain again—*real* rain. It commingles with the smears of blood on the windshield, and the wipers slap it all away. The rain falls harder,

Turn to the next page.

washing not only the windshield clean but the road ahead, the fields, and the entire landscape as well.

"What—was that all about?" Tanya stammers.

Shawn puts his arm around his sister. "I don't know," he says. "But it's all over now." He pats her on the back. "You OK?" he asks.

Tanya nods, but she points ahead. "I'm OK, but it looks like they're not." Up ahead a grisly sight comes into view through the mist of purifying rain. A green-and-white truck, its cab crumpled under its trailer, lays in a twisted heap in the road as smoke streams from beneath the ravaged metal. Police cars and ambulances, their strobe lights slowly turning, are clustered about on the shoulder of the road.

"How terrible!" gasps Mrs. Meyers, slowing as she passes the truck.

As you go by, you see a trail of car parts, glass, and shredded tires littering the wet road. And being carried from the road by two men is a sheared-off panel from the truck. In green lettering are the words: *Grungarten Planzen.*

"That's German for Green Garden Nursery," says your grandfather.

"Wonder how the accident happened," wonders Shawn out loud.

You turn and gaze out the back window of the

Turn to the next page.

car—and horror grips you. You stare at something the others have missed. There is another car involved in the wreck. Mangled, on its side in a culvert, is a car—a large, dark foreign car . . . like the one you are in! From it a body is pulled. As the head lolls to one side your mouth drops as you see the face. It is your own! Unable to speak, you see other bodies laid out on the grass. They are those of Tanya, Shawn, Mrs. Meyers, and your grandfather. Your tongue wags up and down as you try to speak. Your ears register that Shawn is saying something. You look at him in mute horror. Then you stare at the road ahead, knowing what is coming.

The car gathers speed.

You want to tell Mrs. Meyers to slow down. To stop. But you can say nothing. No words seem to be coming from your now useless mouth.

Coming around a bend, out of control, is a large green-and-white truck. You scream as you see the words, *Grungarten Planzen.* You scream again at the wrenching impact, then all goes black.

Your head throbs as you slowly regain consciousness. You are on your back. Your eyes flutter open, and you find yourself in a hospital.

Your grandfather is looking down at you. "You're awake!" he exclaims, tears in his eyes.

Turn to the next page.

"You're OK!" cries Tanya. She hobbles toward a door, and you notice the heavy white walking cast on her leg.

"How do you feel?" asks your grandfather.

You try to answer, but your mouth is too dry. Seeing this, he holds the straw from a glass of water to your lips. You drink thirstily. "Where am I?" you manage to say.

"In a hospital, in Adjud, Romania."

"How did I get here?" you croak.

"You've been in a coma for twelve days. Don't you remember? Don't you remember the accident?"

"But I thought that was just a dream."

"It was no dream," says your grandfather, pulling up a chair and then taking your hand. "Do you remember going on the picnic?" he asks.

You nod, for the first time noticing the bruises on your grandfather's face and the stitches in his chin.

"And do you remember that you, Shawn, and Tanya went hiking up to that cave?"

You nod again.

"Well, after that we were heading back and it started to rain," your grandfather explains.

"Yes, it rained blood," you say.

Your grandfather frowns. His bushy white eyebrows come together as he looks at you in puzzlement.

Turn to the next page.

"Well, maybe in your coma you dreamed that it rained blood, but I assure you, in reality, it was only water."

"Later on in my dream," you say, "the rain of blood turned into ordinary rain and then there was that truck . . . white and green . . . coming right at us . . ."

"Then you *do* remember!" he exclaims, patting your shoulder.

"Just parts of it, I guess," you say. "It's all mixed up and—"

A doctor and a nurse hurry into the room, with Tanya, Shawn, and Mrs. Meyers right behind them. Mrs. Meyers has a brace on her neck, and Shawn's arms are bandaged.

Over her right eye, the doctor flips down a circular mirror with a hole in the middle of it. Her face looms close to yours as a penlight goes on. She aims it first at one eye, then at the other. "That is good," she says in heavily accented English. "You're going to be fine . . . just fine!"

"Stop!" you yell at Mrs. Meyers.

But she isn't listening to you any more than she is to the others. Deafened by fear, she keeps steady pressure on the accelerator. As polka dots of blood spatter the windshield, she leaves the highway and begins a steady ascent along a road winding up into the hills.

"Where are you going, Mom?" begs Tanya.

Mrs. Meyers doesn't answer. Instead she continues along the road that curves around a hill. The rain of blood abates, then suddenly stops altogether. A soft mist of rain—of water—begins to fall, and as it does it washes the blood from the car. The wipers, which once smeared blood back and forth, soon are slapping at pink water, then only at clear liquid.

You pass through a tunnel, and when you emerge you find the town of Adjud directly below, nestled in a valley. In the far distance, crouched in a cleft between two mountains, is the Adjud dam. Mrs. Meyers, with a sigh of relief, pulls the car off to the side of the road and turns off the engine. Instantly the sun breaks through the clouds, bathing the valley, town, and the distant dam in glorious sunshine.

"How pretty!" says Tanya, rolling down a window and pointing at a beautiful rainbow of pastels arching majestically through the faraway mist.

Turn to the next page.

The sun becomes a huge golden disk. The intensity of its heat burns away the rainbow and burns the moisture from the ground. But it doesn't stop there. The sun begins to actually *cook* the land, desiccating it completely. Suddenly the sun takes its toll on the dam—and like the ground, it begins to crack . . . and then it collapses altogether!

In horror you watch a great wall of blood-red liquid set free . . . heading for the town below. You look down at the people, miniaturized by distance, staring in mute terror at what used to be a dam—at what is now a towering wall of blood rushing down the valley.

Within minutes it hits the town, spreading in all directions in a vicious wave of foaming red. Booming down streets, it tosses and buckles and breaks cars, buses, and trucks in its path as if they were toys.

"What do we do?" screams Shawn in panic.

But there is nothing you can do but sit, watch, and wait, as a second great wave of blood rolls over the first and thunders toward the already destroyed town.

The continuous sound of collapsing buildings and smashing glass mixes with the screams of people and animals being swept along in the torrent. Cries of terror reach your ears from the town below.

As the horrible wave comes to a juncture where

Turn to the next page.

the valley abruptly narrows, it crashes back upon itself, sending great geysers of blood into the air. Finally the horrid river slows, then settles, forming a vast lake of blood covering the town almost completely. Rapidly the red waters begin to rise.

"We have to get out of here!" you yell.

Mrs. Meyers has already restarted the engine. She is backing the car away from the rising red lake . . . but blood is already spilling over the road ahead, sweeping toward you, hissing like an incoming tide. It swirls and slaps against a cliff, then against the car, and still continues to rise.

The car's engine dies.

All of you are screaming. You roll up the windows as the blood rises higher and higher, roiling up and turning the glass red. Then all goes dark in the car as the crimson horror engulfs the entire vehicle.

Too late, you realize your window is open just a hair. Blood spurts through the tiny opening, wetting your neck and face. You try to wipe it off, but before you do, your tongue accidentally touches it. It is sweet, surprisingly sweet and good. You close your eyes, actually delighting in the taste of the blood. More of the sweet liquid splashes on you.

"Stop it!" yells Tanya.

Your eyes snap open. You sit up, and find yourself

Turn to the next page.

on the picnic blanket.

"That's enough, Shawn!" yells Mrs. Meyers. "You're getting it all over everybody."

You blink, then blink again. Shawn has a bottle of cherry cola. He has been shaking up the bottle and squirting his sister—and inadvertently spraying you and everyone else. He is about to shake up the bottle again when his mother takes it from him.

"What's going on?" you mutter.

Your grandfather has a napkin in his hand and is wiping red soda pop off your face. "You dozed off during my story," he says, turning your head with his hand and wiping soda off your neck.

"Sorry you had such a rude awakening," says Mrs. Meyers, casting an accusatory look at Shawn.

"Sorry," he says to you. "I didn't mean to get any on you. I was just trying to get Tanya."

"No big deal," you say with a smile, filled with relief to find yourself out of your bloody nightmare and tasting sweet reality.

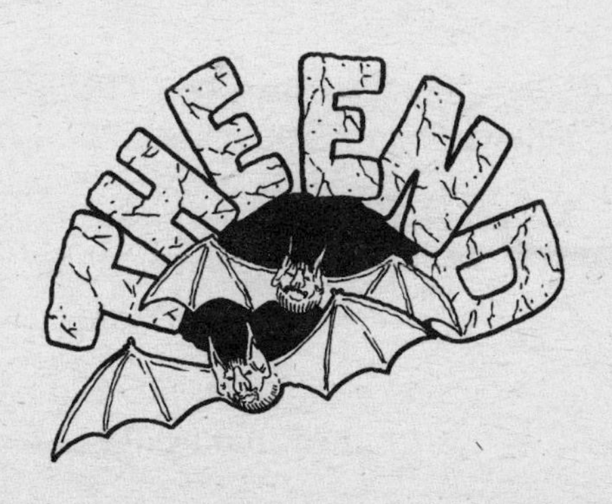

You head up, relieved to find that the way ahead is illuminated by light streaming through cracks and fissures high overhead in the stony ceiling. The stairs end abruptly, and you discover that you are on a large, circular landing of well-worn stone. Directly ahead is a dark tunnel. To your right are steel elevator doors. On the wall next to them is a button and an arrow pointing up.

If you push the button opening the elevator doors, turn to the ***next page****.*

If you continue on into the tunnel, turn to ***page 121****.*

"Going up?" you ask your friends with a smile, trying to be funny.

But Tanya and Shawn look dead serious. It is clear they are not too happy about being stuck in someone else's dream.

You push the button outside the elevator, and as the heavy doors roll open, the three of you enter. On the display panel before you are the numbers 1 through 7.

"It's your dream," Shawn says, shrugging. "So it's your pick."

*If you push 1, turn to the **next page**.*

*If you push 2, turn to **page 81**.*

*If you push 3, turn to **page 82**.*

*If you push 4, turn to **page 91**.*

*If you push 5, turn to **page 92**.*

*If you push 6, turn to **page 103**.*

*If you push 7, turn to **page 108**.*

"Number 1 is as good as any," you say, and after you push the button, the elevator doors close, then open into the lobby of your hotel!

"Hey, how'd we get here?" you ask, turning to look back at your friends. But the elevator is empty!

The hair rising on the back of your neck, you enter the lobby. Across the way is your grandfather.

"Grandfather!" you exclaim, running up to him. "Have you seen Tanya and Shawn?"

"Who?" he asks, frowning. "Are you feeling OK?"

"Yes! I feel fine, but—"

Suddenly you stop yourself. Entering the lobby's revolving doors are your friends and their mother.

"Shawn! Tanya! Mrs. Meyers!" you say happily.

"Huh?" says Tanya.

"Who are you?" asks Shawn.

Mrs. Meyers furrows her brow. "And how did you know our names?"

You stare at these people who have obviously never met you before, and who you have met . . . but only in your dreams.

"Just for kicks let's skip 1 and go for 2," you say, and pushing the button, you quickly ascend.

When the door opens, your grandfather stands there. He smiles and you scream. His teeth are razor-sharp fangs!

"Grandfather!" you cry, but he says nothing. Behind you, Tanya and Shawn giggle.

"That is not your grandfather," says Tanya.

"You are such a fool!" bellows Shawn, his breath rotten and reeking of death.

Slowly you turn and gag in revulsion at the two corpses before you that a moment ago had been your friends. Now their bony hands are clamping onto you.

"Welcome the Prince of Darkness!" Shawn and Tanya demand in unison. "Give to him your blood as we have!"

Stunned, you try to struggle, but before you know it you feel the twin stabs of pain and the warm flow of your blood leaving your body, as the vampire that your grandfather has become drains the life out of you.

You push 3. The heavy doors roll shut, but the elevator does not ascend. Instead the steel wall behind you slowly rolls up to reveal a mine shaft.

Confused, the three of you make your way down the long, winding shaft until you come upon an old man. Looking deathly pale, he lies propped against the wall of the mine. Several canteens and three canvas bags are at his side. Though it is extremely warm in the mine, the old man is shivering uncontrollably. He looks up and tries to speak, but breaks into a fit of ragged coughing.

"Are you sick?" you ask. "Can we help you?"

"Can't," he gasps. "I'm dyin'. A cave-in killed my mule and crushed my ribs and back. I've been lying here for days in the middle of this desert."

"Desert?" you ask. Making your way to the mouth of the cave, you gaze out at rocks and sand. "Where are we?" you ask, returning into the mine.

"Harquahala Mountains," he says. "In Arizona."

"Arizona?" you blurt. "How could we be there?"

"Don't rightly know," says the old man weakly. "But that's where you are. And this is the Tipton Mine. Lloyd Tipton's my name."

"What's in the bags?" asks Tanya, studying the canvas bags on the ground.

"Gold, young lady. I worked this old mine most of

Turn to the next page.

my life. Finally struck it rich." He smiles sardonically. "And now here I am, dying."

"Gold?" the three of you gasp.

"Yep, gold," rasps the old man. "Might as well take it," he says, his voice a grating whisper.

"You mean it?" asks Shawn, his eyes gleaming.

"Of course he does!" exclaims Tanya. Pushing in front of you and Shawn, she opens a bag and runs her fingers over the shimmering nuggets.

Watching her, the old man cackles, then looks up at you. "Worth a lot of money," he coaxes. "Millions!"

You kneel down beside the gold. Like your friends, you feel its power, lure, and beauty. Slowly a change—perhaps greed, or something more evil—seems to consume every fiber of your being.

Suddenly a horrific fit of coughing and hacking comes from the old man. Briefly taking your eyes off the gold, you glance over at him. Preoccupied, feeling oddly indifferent now to his plight, you watch as he takes a huge, heaving breath, then goes limp.

"He's dead," you say matter-of-factly.

Shawn shrugs and smiles crookedly. "The gold's all ours now! We each get a third."

You nod, eyeing him suspiciously as he begins to check the sacks.

"What're you looking at?" he demands. "I'm just

Turn to the next page.

seeing if the gold is distributed equally."

But since you and Tanya don't trust him, you both help Shawn check the sacks. Then each of you slings a sack over one shoulder and a canteen over the other, and the three of you set off across the desert. In the far distance you can make out a tiny dot that appears to be a town.

"Looks like it's miles from here," you say.

"We'll make it," Tanya snarls. "At least *I* will!"

In silence, the three of you pick your way across a boulder-strewn slope. Deep down, you know the gold has changed all of you, but you don't care. All that matters to you now is the wealth you carry on your back.

You are the first to see the rattlesnake coiled on a boulder. Shawn is walking right toward it, not seeing it since his eyes are on the ground. You could warn him, but instead you wait for the snake to strike.

The snake arches back, then sinks its fangs into Shawn's leg. His shrieks shattering the desert silence, he falls to his knees, then onto his back, grabbing hold of the creature with both hands. Its tail loops around his arms, and it strikes again, locking its fangs onto Shawn's neck. Crying for help, Shawn looks back and forth in terror from you to his sister.

You look at Tanya and she looks at you. A strange

Turn to the next page.

smile comes over her face, and you know she is thinking the same thing you are: Shawn is beyond help, and soon all the gold in his pack will be yours to split.

It is only a matter of moments before the venom takes its deadly toll. You and Tanya watch dispassionately as Shawn begins to walk in circles, mumbling over and over, "I'm rich" . . . until he draws his last breath.

Like vultures, you and Tanya descend on Shawn's motionless body—or rather, on his sack of gold. Finally you divide it equally and split the water in his canteen. Then, heartlessly, you leave Shawn's body to rot in the desert sun.

As the blazing sun rises higher in the sky, sweat pours from you, and the now heavier sack of gold seems to be pulling you right down into the earth. Slowly you begin to sag with the effort, and your mind grows dim, as though your brain is practically broiled by the heat. Now you must stop for water every few steps.

The heat is also taking a heavy toll on Tanya. Repeatedly she takes long gulps from her canteen.

The two of you stop and rest. You open your backpack and gaze at all the gold there. The sight of it fills you with extraordinary pleasure. You look out

Turn to the next page.

across the desert and see that the town is considerably closer now.

I'm going to make it! you tell yourself. I'm going to be rich!

You notice Tanya looking at you. For so long she has seemed sullen, suspicious, and mean-spirited. But she is smiling now.

"I've decided something," she says.

"What?" you ask wearily.

"I really don't need all this gold." She shrugs. "Not this much, anyway."

Miserable from heat and thirst, feeling light-headed and having difficulty comprehending what she's getting at, you study Tanya and wait for her to go on.

"Tell you what," she says. "You've still got plenty of water. I'll trade you a fourth of my gold for a drink of water." She studies you eagerly. "Is it a deal?"

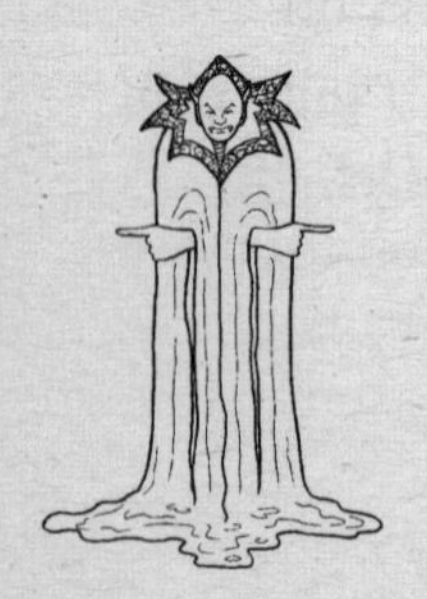

If you make the trade,
*turn to the **next page**.*

If you don't make the trade,
*turn to **page 90**.*

For Tanya to trade all that gold for water, her mind must be totally gone, you muse.

"Well?" demands Tanya.

"I think you're crazy," you say, "but you've got yourself a deal!"

The exchange is made, and you continue on your way as the fierce sun seems to suck every bit of strength from you. Glare from the glistening white sand all but blinds you, and shimmering waves of heat bend and distort the air, making the far-off town seem to be doing some kind of dance. Your breath comes in overheated, little gasps and your legs feel like wooden posts, making your footfalls leaden.

Tanya stops in her tracks and takes several gulps of water. You follow suit. Then Tanya shakes her canteen and frowns. She tosses the empty canteen to the sand. Grinning at her, you shake yours and hear a reassuring slosh inside.

"I need more water," says Tanya.

"So I see."

"Please," she begs.

"All right," you say, "but the price has doubled: Half of your gold for one drink of my water."

"I'll do better than that," she says. "I'll give you *all* my gold for whatever water you've got left."

You eye her then look in the direction of the

Turn to the next page.

town. The place is now only a few miles away.

"Is it a deal?" she asks.

"Yeah," you say with a grin.

You hand Tanya the canteen, as she in turn loads the rest of her gold into your backpack.

The two of you continue on. But soon, burdened by the great weight on your back, you begin to lag behind. Tanya, on the other hand, carrying nothing but the canteen, moves along at a steady pace, now and then taking a drink.

"Please," you call. "Tanya, please let me have just a little water."

She pauses briefly. "No," she says. "The deal's been made."

You hang your head, too weary to even respond, and begin plodding on, the town now only a few hundred yards away. Almost there! you tell yourself. Got to hang on—just a little longer. But you are staggering now, reeling, your head throbbing, your tongue lolling in your mouth. Suddenly, as though your legs have melted, you drop to the sand. You try to rise, then fall again, the weight of the gold pinning you to the earth.

You hear the swishing sound of footsteps on the sand, and gazing up blearily, see Tanya coming back to you.

Turn to the next page.

"Help me," you beg, your voice a feeble, dry croak.

She grins, takes a long drink, and then, tossing the canteen to the ground, comes around behind you. She pulls the backpack off you, then hoists it onto her own shoulders.

What are you doing? you want to say. But you are too weak to utter a word. Still somewhere, deep in the recesses of your hazy mind, you understand all too well what Tanya is doing—and has been doing to you all along.

"Thank you," she says, leering cruelly at you. "Thank you for the water—and for carrying all my gold across the desert for me."

"You greedy little . . ." you rasp, but your voice cracks. Saying more is now impossible.

"No more greedy than you . . . just smarter." She chuckles. "And your greed will be the death of you."

Lying on the burning sand, the last bit of life ebbing from your body, you see Tanya head away . . . on the last short leg of the journey to the town.

"No," you say, as if coming out of the trance. "It isn't a deal. Out here, water is precious. Gold is worthless."

"But I don't have any more water!" cries Tanya.

You drop your pack full of gold to the sand. "Tell you what," you say. "I have a deal for *you*. We'll share my water and walk to town. Both of us will leave our gold out here. Maybe it'll be here when we get back, maybe it won't. But at least this way we'll both survive."

For a long moment Tanya stares at you. "It makes sense," she finally says as if she, too, has come out of a trance. She lets her pack drop to the sand, and together the two of you head for town.

Halfway there, Tanya turns to you. "I don't know how this nightmare of yours will end," she tells you. "But at least we'll be going there together."

"Let's give number 4 a try," you say with a shrug.

At first, nothing seems to happen. But then, to your horror, the walls begin to move—inward.

Terrified, the three of you throw yourselves against the walls and push, but the walls continue to close in on you. And now to your horror, you see that the ceiling is descending, and you feel the floor rising!

Shrieking, as your arms and legs become tangled with those of your friends, you feel as though you are being crushed, and then . . . you wake up, face down on a picnic blanket!

With the wind knocked out of your lungs, you sit up and find your arms and legs tangled with those of your friends. Slowly you realize what is going on. While you were having your horrid nightmare, Tanya and Shawn, who were wrestling, fell on top of you.

"Oops!" Tanya yelps. "Sorry, sleepyhead. Shawn and I were just messing around."

"Yeah," Shawn says. "We didn't mean to wake you."

"No problem," you say, laughing, filled with relief. "No problem at all!"

You push 5. The elevator ascends. It comes to a stop and opens onto a dark, snaking tunnel.

Tanya peers inside. "Not another tunnel!" she exclaims. "I wonder where this one leads."

"There's only one way to find out," you say, heading off into the tunnel with Tanya and Shawn right behind you.

Rounding a bend, you find that the tunnel walls are really rounded walls of concrete, and soon you realize that you are not in a tunnel but in a large storm drain. Ahead is a yellow flickering neon light.

As the three of you hurry along, you are gradually bathed in the glow of the yellow light. Then, to your amazement, you find yourself walking right into what appears to be an office!

Sitting at a modern desk, behind an outdated computer, is a stoop-shouldered man. He swivels in his chair at your approaching footsteps, weak blue eyes gazing up at you over wire-rimmed glasses.

"And who might you be?" he asks.

Fidgeting and looking around the ultramodern office, you tell him your names.

"I am Mr. Skalaka," he says. "Have you come here for foresight?"

"Foresight?" you ask, puzzled.

"Knowledge of one's future," Mr. Skalaka explains.

Turn to the next page.

He pushes his glasses higher on his nose. "And the question I must put to you is whether or not this is something you wish to know."

"How much does it cost?" Shawn asks.

"No money, although there *is* a price to pay."

"And that price is?" Tanya asks skeptically.

"The price you pay is determined by what you learn," Mr. Skalaka says flatly.

"And what kinds of things will we learn?" you ask.

"You will find out if your future is to be a happy one or not," he answers with a slight grin. "I can tell you how long you will live and how and when you will die."

"How neat!" exclaims Shawn.

"And frightening," you add.

Mr. Skalaka leans back in his reclining desk chair, studying the three of you. "What is your decision?" he asks. "Do you wish to know your future?"

"Well?" asks Shawn, turning to you.

"You decide," says Tanya. "If you do it, so will we."

*If you decide to know your future, turn to the **next page**.*

*If you decide not to, turn to **page 102**.*

The urge to know is just too irresistible. "OK," you tell Mr. Skalaka, "please tell us our futures."

He nods and turns to his rather odd, ancient-looking computer. "I will need to know your full names, ages, and the places and dates of your birth."

"My full name is—" you begin.

"Excuse me for interrupting," says Tanya, "but I have one more question before we start."

"Which is?" Mr. Skalaka asks, raising an eyebrow.

"Knowing our lives in advance, can we change any of it in any way?"

"No, I'm afraid not." He poises his fingers over the keyboard. "Please proceed."

First you, then Shawn and Tanya, relay the information asked for as Mr. Skalaka enters it into the computer. Then he pushes a control button, and the question *REVEAL CODES?* appears on the monitor. Mr. Skalaka taps out the word *yes*, then punches *PRINT*, and leans back as the obsolete-looking piece of equipment prints out three pages. Picking them up, he frowns as he reads the few brief lines on each piece of paper.

"Wha-what do they say?" asks Shawn nervously.

But Mr. Skalaka turns away from Shawn and looks at Tanya.

"Your future, young lady," he says, "is quite a

Turn to the next page.

bright one. You will overcome an early trauma to lead a long, good, and productive life. You will have a successful career. You will marry at the age of 32, have one child, and live to be 87. Your death will be peaceful and of natural causes—of a cerebral hemorrhage, to be exact."

"Well," says Tanya, smiling, "that sounds pretty good, even though the cerebral hemorrhage part is kind of scary."

"How about me?" you blurt.

"And me?" asks Shawn, biting his nails.

"I'm sorry," he says softly, turning to the two of you.

"Sorry?" you mumble, suddenly worried.

"It—it's usually not this bad," says the stoop-shouldered little man.

"Tell us!" you beg.

He ignores Shawn and studies you sadly, blinks, and scans the paper. "Your life will be one of grief and torment, of isolation and madness. You will die at the age of 27—exactly 4,748 days from now—at 3:32 P.M. on a Friday, in Sibu, Romania."

"Die of *what*?" you implore, horror coursing through every fiber of your being.

"General atrophy of the organs, though the direct cause of death will be renal failure brought about by years of taking potent anti-psychotic drugs."

Turn to the next page.

"*Anti-psychotic!* You mean, I'm going to go crazy?"

Mr. Skalaka nods. "You will be institutionalized at various facilities for a period of thirteen years for catatonic depression."

"You're wrong!" you blurt. "There's nothing wrong with my mind! I'm not insane!"

Mr. Skalaka looks at you with pity in his eyes. "But I'm afraid you soon will be. I'm afraid that when—"

"And me?" interrupts Shawn, his face taut with apprehension.

"Your fate, young man, oddly interwoven with that of your friend, is more dreadful. The only consolation I can offer you is that your demise will not be so long and drawn out, not protracted over the years."

"How will I die?" Shawn asks, his voice a feeble whisper. He begins to tremble.

"You will be crushed to death."

"No!" yells Shawn. "You're just making this up! You're wrong!"

Mr. Skalaka says nothing.

"Whe-when will my brother . . . die?" stammers Tanya, her lips trembling.

He looks at the paper. "In twenty-nine minutes."

Tears in his eyes, chin quivering, Shawn stares at

Turn to the next page.

Mr. Skalaka. "You're saying I'll be dead in less than half an hour! And it will be over quickly and—?"

"Yes, you have only a short while to live. But *no*—though it will happen suddenly, I'm afraid it will not be over quickly."

"That doesn't make any sense!" screams Shawn.

"He's crazy, Shawn!" you yell. "Don't pay any attention to him!"

"Yeah," says Tanya, putting a hand on your shoulder, trying to keep you calm. "He is crazy. Don't worry, Shawn. Don't even *think* about what he said." Glaring angrily at Mr. Skalaka, she takes Shawn's elbow. "Come on. Let's get out of here!"

"You've got my vote!" exclaims Shawn.

Together the three of you run headlong from the room and back into the maze of concrete pipes. Making blind turn after blind turn, you suddenly find yourself entering a tunnel of natural rock, and directly ahead, no more than fifty meters away, is an opening through which daylight streams.

"An exit!" you exclaim.

"Great!" pants Shawn, a few steps behind you and Tanya.

You glance back at Shawn, and are suddenly terrified to see that in his haste he has accidentally bumped into a jagged rock projecting loosely from

Turn to the next page.

the side of the tunnel wall. The rock tumbles free and as it does, a jumble of sodden earth and heavy stones collapses with a roar.

"Shawn!" you scream, looking back as the small avalanche thunders down onto your friend, proving Mr. Skalaka's prophecy to be true.

But almost in the same instant you see something that fills you with an overwhelming sense of relief. Though coughing and a bit dazed, Shawn suddenly materializes out of the dust and rushes into your arms!

"He was wrong!" Shawn shouts. "I was *almost* crushed, but I'm alive!"

The sudden toppling of another slag of stone behind you and the hiss of cascading gravel again fills you with apprehension—and propels you into action. Grabbing Shawn and Tanya's hands, pulling them into motion, the three of you take off at a loping run down the tunnel. A moment later you find yourself emerging from the cave into bright sunshine.

You hear someone calling your name.

Shielding your eyes against the glare of the sun, you make out your grandfather and another man standing on a platform abutting a wooden structure built out over a stream. Your grandfather waves, and you and your friends wave back as you hurry down to where they are waiting.

Turn to the next page.

"Where've you three been?" asks your grandfather, a strident tone to his voice. "I've been looking all over for you."

"We got lost in the cave," you explain.

"Where's my mom?" asks Tanya.

"Waiting back at the car, just over that ridge," answers your grandfather, pointing. "She has been worried sick."

"I'll go tell her we're all right," says Tanya.

"Good idea," says your grandfather. Then as Tanya hurries off, he launches into a lecture, scolding both you and Shawn for getting lost. Suddenly he stops himself and puts a hand on the man beside him. "Please forgive my manners," he says. "This is Vaclav."

You and Shawn say hello.

The man, old and white haired, nods.

"Vaclav runs the mill here," says your grandfather. "He was helping me look for you kids."

"Perhaps you would enjoy to come and rest a moment?" asks the man in faltering, heavily accented English. "And maybe you like food refreshments?"

"Yes, thank you," you say, and then you, Shawn, and your grandfather follow him as he leads you into the mill.

Entering, you hear the rhythmic slop and splash of

Turn to the next page.

a tall waterwheel. And connected to it is a whirling drive shaft slowly turning a heavy, circular grindstone.

Vaclav finds an apple in a small basket and, producing a knife from his belt, proceeds to slice it in half. Cutting out the seeds and core, he offers a portion to you and Shawn. With a smile, Shawn reaches for it . . . as the sleeve of his shirt brushes against two bolts protruding from the spinning shaft. He screams, as more of his clothing, then his arm, is pulled into the grinding machinery.

Your screams echo those of your friend, as he now is sucked slowly into the turning shaft. Vaclav, the elderly man, stumbles to a hand brake and pulls down on it with all his might, and the machine comes to a clattering halt. But it is too late. In numb horror you approach Shawn, to where he is twisted into the machinery, horribly crushed to death.

You start shrieking . . . and do not stop.

* * *

Thirteen years later, in the Kiselev Institute for the Emotionally Disturbed, in Sibu, Romania, you lie coiled in a tight knot on your bed. Now and then a doctor or a nurse looks in on you. Sometimes they try to get you to speak, but you have not spoken since you saw Shawn crushed to death.

Turn to the next page.

Your skin is pale and waxy, and your eyes are unfocused. You think only of Shawn—see only him—so many years ago, going around and around, being crushed to death. Sometimes in your mind you see Mr. Skalaka—and even hear his voice, telling you that you will go insane.

Your eyes move slowly in their shrinking sockets. There is no calendar or clock on the wall. There is no obvious way of knowing how long you have been in this place. But lying there, you have outsmarted them all. You've been counting the days, mentally ticking off your birthdays. No one is there to tell you. No one needs to. You are 27 years old. It is a Friday. And it is 3:31 P.M. You feel the sickness within you, the anguish, and the relief of knowing you have only one more minute to live.

"No," you say, "I think knowledge of the future—our future—is simply something we're better off not having."

Mr. Skalaka looks to you, then back to his computer. His fingers play across the keyboard. He punches a key, waits, tears off a printout, and reads.

"What does it say?" you ask.

Mr. Skalaka smiles. "That, my friend," he says, "is now something for me to know and you to find out."

Turn back to the choices on page 79.

You push the 6 button and immediately realize the horrible mistake you've made as the floor of the elevator drops open like a trap door, and you, Shawn, and Tanya plummet through black space. Shimmering black wetness seems to rush up at you, and a fraction of a second later you slam face-first into warm, wretched-smelling water.

You flail at the disgusting stuff, stroking with all your strength in an effort to rise back to the surface. Finally you break through, and near gagging, you take in huge gulps of air. And then you look about, calling frantically for your friends. But there is no answer.

Treading water and turning circles in the horrid pond of inklike fluid, you see only the great black body of water into which you've fallen. If there is a shore to this putrid, underground lake, you cannot see it.

"Shawn!" you cry out again. "Tanya!"

As if in response, there is a noisy upwelling of black bubbles a short distance from you. Below a form takes shape, a human form, eyes glowing like two underwater stars. With a loud burst a head breaks the surface and shoulders emerge, and you find yourself staring not at your friends, but at a corpse! Its flesh is a ghastly white-yellow, its eyes a luminous green.

As you scream, the corpse opens *its* mouth and

Turn to the next page.

screams back at you—in *your* voice. Paralyzed with horror and helpless, you gape as more corpselike forms break the surface of the black water.

With a shriek you break free of your paralyzing fear and frantically stroke away toward the dark outline of what appears to be a shoreline. As you swim, more corpses bob into view on each side of you. Oddly enough, they reach out at you, but make no attempt at pursuit.

The shore looms closer, and you hear the gentle slap of waves breaking against it. Light-headed from exhaustion, and with every muscle in your body throbbing, you struggle on, your back kick feeble, your arm strokes weak. You are almost to shore when suddenly you hear a cry somewhere behind you . . . and then another. The voices are familiar.

"Help me!" wails Tanya.

"Please! Help!" cries Shawn. "We're drowning."

Your first instinct is to swim to them, to save them. But you are so tired you're not even sure if you have the strength to reach them. But these are your friends. You should try to save them. How can you just leave them, ignoring their cries for help?

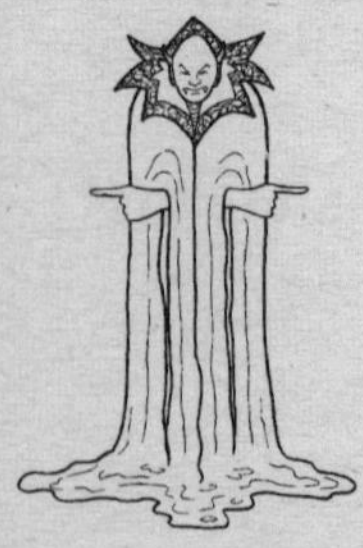

*If you swim back out after your friends, turn to the **next page**.*

*If you find it impossible to swim out after them, turn to **page 109**.*

Even knowing that you may die in the attempt, you cannot abandon your friends, and you begin swimming back out into the warm, foul-smelling water. Slowly you close in on them. Their cries get louder, nearer, and soon you can see them clearly. Their faces filled with fear, they are grabbing onto one another, at the same time holding onto a rotted, water-soaked log.

"Help us!" cries Shawn.

"We can't swim!" sobs Tanya.

You are gasping as you struggle toward them. You stroke with arms of lead and legs of wood. And suddenly you are seized with fierce cramps! First your thigh muscles tighten painfully, then the cramp spreads to your abdomen, squeezing your stomach muscles into an excruciating knot. You try to fight it, but it is hopeless.

"Hang on!" yells Shawn.

It is the last thing you hear before your head sinks beneath the surface. Your mind goes as black as the water in which you slowly descend. In a last bid for life, your body screaming for oxygen, you open your mouth wide to suck in air, but instead inhale the putrid water. As you begin to drown, your heart throbs in your chest, louder . . . harder . . . faster . . . and suddenly it seems to explode.

Turn to the ***next page.***

Dead, your body drifts to the bottom of the lake. And though you do not feel it, know nothing of it, your feet touch the muck of the lake bottom. Then your body slowly topples backward, and settles on its side in the foul, viscous silt.

Oblivious to all, dark forms are walking across the lake bottom toward where you lie. The hand of a corpse touches you. Then there are more hands, as the corpses who inhabit this underwater hell pull your lifeless body upright. One corpse embraces you, plants its rotted mouth on your lips, and breathes the life of the living dead into you.

Suddenly your dead eyes open underwater, and though you can not see them, they are shining a luminous green just like the eyes of the corpses that surround you. The corpses smile. And you smile in return—a dark, twisted smile—as you answer the command of your dormant brain. It tells you to rise in the black water.

As your head breaks the surface, Tanya screams. "It can't be!" Your radiant, green eyes shine brighter at her.

"You're dead!" screams Shawn.

More of the black forms bob into view, all around the three of you. First there are only a few. Then there are hundreds bobbing up all about.

Turn to the next page.

Tanya and Shawn are hysterical with fear. They are trying to get away from the corpses . . . and away from you. But they cannot leave the log that supports them, and if they did, where could they go in this corpse-filled black lake?

You reach out and touch Shawn's face with dead, slimy fingers.

He flinches, recoils in horror. "Leave me alone!" he shrieks.

"Leave me alone!" you repeat, in his voice.

"Why are you doing this?" cries Tanya.

"Why are you doing this?" you shout back, now in *her* voice.

You begin to laugh . . . the laugh of the dead. And then to the accompaniment of Shawn and Tanya's screams, all the other corpses cackle as your friends are about to meet the same fate as yours . . . only *they* will die to the sounds of an orchestra of nightmarish laughter.

"My lucky number is 7," says Tanya. "Try it."

"OK," you say, and after pushing the button, everything goes black. In the darkness you hear Tanya, who has just told you to press 7, asking, "Why seven?" Then you hear your grandfather reply, "I don't know."

You blink. Then blink again. Blinking a third time, you open your eyes to find yourself lying on the picnic blanket. Your grandfather is talking, and Tanya, Shawn, and Mrs. Meyers are listening attentively to what he is saying.

"I only know," continues your grandfather, "that according to vampire legend, the seventh son of a seventh son always turns into a vampire. The same is said to be the fate of those born with teeth."

"I wish it hadn't been a seven," says Tanya. "Now I feel creepy having seven be my lucky number."

"Then get yourself a new stupid lucky number!" says Shawn, rolling his eyes.

You smile to yourself. Seven worked pretty good for me, you muse. It just got me out of one horrible nightmare!

You want desperately to go after your friends, but you know it is impossible. You are dizzy, and your muscles are knotted, cramping, and twisting up into horridly painful knots. It is all you can do to reach the shore.

Gasping, you slosh and stagger from the water then collapse on the mucky, black beach. Panting, sick with exhaustion and fear, you struggle to your feet and gaze out at the water. All is empty, silent. Tanya and Shawn are gone. You cry their names again and again, but there is no answer. The only thing alive in this wet, grotesque hell appears to be you.

Sobbing, you stumble to higher ground. You gaze at the black lake, then follow the dark shoreline trailing off into the darkness around it. Behind you is a low-lying hill, with a narrow trail zigzagging up its barren slope.

Which way should you head? Does either choice hold any hope of finding your friends?

If you climb the hill,
turn to the ***next page.***

If you decide to follow the shoreline
winding around the lake,
turn to ***page 114.***

Climbing the hill, you are surprised to see dark rain clouds with sunlight streaming through them—*inside* a cave. Your surprise grows as you see that directly below is a normal-looking town.

You hurry down the slope and soon find yourself on a paved highway, walking along the side of the road. Within minutes you are entering what appears to be a midwestern town. Cars and trucks whisk past on rain-dampened streets. There are many pedestrians about, most of whom are attired in rain gear.

"Excuse me, ma'am," you say, approaching an elderly lady in a pink raincoat. "What town is this?"

"Tecumseh, Nebraska," she replies.

After thanking her, you continue on your way, noticing how strangely heavy and still the air is. It feels as though it is pressing down on you. And though it is clearly daytime, the sky is rapidly turning black as night.

"Have you ever seen weather like this?" you hear a man outside a grocery store asking a man wearing a food-checker's apron.

"Never," replies the man, gazing up at the dark sky. "And I don't like the looks of it."

All of a sudden it begins to rain. But the drops aren't hitting the street. They are flying sideways! With the rain comes an odd roaring noise. Above the roar

Turn to the next page.

you hear the sharp tinkling of breaking glass. You turn in time to see a mailbox flying by. It passes just inches from your head, causing you to dive to the ground.

"Tornado!" you hear someone scream, as a stop sign somersaults through the air.

The wind is overwhelming, unlike anything you've ever known. You grab hold of a pole, afraid that at any moment you will be torn from the pole and sucked up into the black sky.

As you cling for dear life, a powerful force begins to come down the street, ripping the fronts off buildings and shattering glass in its wake. One place after another simply explodes. Power lines tear loose, showering sparks everywhere. People run, ducking and stumbling for cover. Cars brake and swerve away from them. One is flipped by the force of the wind and rolls sideways, tumbling over and over until it crashes through a plate glass window.

You try to get inside the open door of a building, but the wind has you glued to the pole.

Out of the corner of your eye you see a mail carrier pressed against the wall of a building, screaming, trying to hold onto the wall with his fingertips. An instant later he is pulled away, looking like a human kite, a kite that will never come back, its string broken.

You put your head down against your chest and

*Turn to the **next page.***

feel as though you are going to suffocate. The air is being torn from your lungs. Gasping, you blow in and out, struggling to catch your breath. All the air in the world is apparently being sucked into the tornado.

You look up and can see the ugly, swirling tip of the terrible twister. It dips and sways down the street, demolishing one area and leaving others untouched. It completely misses a hotel across from you but later levels a movie theater. Then it catches a department store and tears away the top four floors. Furniture, clothes, toys, and appliances whirl upward and come apart in the air, landing in pieces blocks away. Roofs are popping off buildings. Giant walls are collapsing like building blocks.

Directly across the way, the wind tears all four walls and the roof off an office building. You see a woman huddled under her desk. Suddenly she runs to where a hallway had been just a few seconds before, and before she can stop herself, the wind carries her out into empty space.

As you listen to her screams, a powerful new eddy of wind hits *you*! Still clinging to the pole, you feel your feet being lifted off the ground, and suddenly you are fluttering like a flag, attached to the pole at a right angle. The gale-force wind pummels you, and all at once you are ripped from the pole,

Turn to the next page.

rocketing out of control toward a brick wall!

As you slam into it, then through it, you land in what appears to be a clothing store. Tangled in fabric, covered with debris, you struggle to free yourself. And then you hear someone calling your name.

You open your eyes to find Shawn and Tanya looking down at you. Your grandfather and Mrs. Meyers are busily packing things up.

"Better get going, sleepyhead," your grandfather says. "It's going to pour."

You are tangled up in a blanket at the picnic site. The sky is black, a blustery wind is blowing, and a scattering of large, dime-sized drops of rain are already falling.

"You fell asleep," says Tanya.

"And this storm started brewing a little while ago," adds Shawn. He looks up, then shields his face from the rain. "It's only gonna get worse," he says. "Looks like our little picnic is over."

"And so is my nightmare!" you exclaim, sitting up and smiling, filled with relief.

Is it possible, you wonder, that Tanya and Shawn somehow made it from the water alive? Or maybe they didn't, and their bodies washed ashore? Either way, whether they are alive or dead, you decide you must make an effort to find them, and the trail around the lake offers the only hope.

Wearily you begin following the shoreline. The footing is vile and wet. Mud sucks at your feet, and it smells so bad it is like walking through a sewer. You slog through rotting vegetation as snails crack under your feet, and slugs and worms crush into a loathsome goo.

Sickened, you are thinking of turning back, when suddenly you discern movement ahead. You see the flash of flesh-colored forms in the eerie gloom. Your heart leaps for joy as Tanya and Shawn lumber toward you!

"We thought you were dead!" cries Shawn, as the three of you embrace. "We kicked ashore holding onto a log. We kept looking for you, but we'd given up."

"There are corpses in that water!" you exclaim.

Tanya nods. "But . . . but now they're not *in* the water, they're *on* it!" She points with a trembling finger at the black lake.

"They're back!" screams Shawn.

Tanya is grabbing you as the three of you back

Turn to the next page.

away from the amazing sight. Walking across the water—on top of the water—are corpses, legions of them . . . and they are headed directly at you.

Too terrified to speak, the three of you turn to run back down the shore. But you stop almost before you start. Down the way you have just come, corpses are emerging everywhere into view, approaching on land as well as on water. With no other choice, you run along the shoreline toward where you hope you will find no corpses.

Skirting huge, sodden boulders growing up out of the muck, you find yourself approaching great heaps of slag that form the entrance to a cave. Looking over your shoulder at the living dead, who relentlessly approach with arms outstretched, you hurry with your friends into the cave.

At first the dark place has high ceilings, but suddenly the cavern tapers, becoming little more than a narrow, corkscrewing crawl space. Sharp, sandpapery rocks scrape against you as you crawl, miserable and in pain, through the tiny space. Disoriented, with all sense of direction gone and all hope evaporating, you wonder if there is any purpose for you to keep struggling. Then suddenly, miraculously, the way ahead broadens, opening into a great, long tunnel.

Filled with renewed hope, you race down it and

Turn to the next page.

are surprised to see torches attached to the walls. A chill descends down your spine, however, as you see there are dozens of coffins lining the tunnel as well.

You quicken your pace—and suddenly from behind, you hear the sound of wood scraping against wood. You turn around to see dead hands pushing the coffin lids aside . . . and dead, waxy bodies stepping from the caskets. Their luminous eyes on you, the corpses slowly begin to come after you, soon joined by the living dead from the lake, who are slithering out of the crawl space and into the tunnel.

The three of you run screaming in abject horror, and each time you pass a coffin, it, too, springs open, releasing its dead, moldering occupant.

"They're everywhere!" screams Tanya.

"Just keep running!" cries Shawn.

Rounding a turn in the tunnel, the three of you come to a stairway. Racing up it, you find blood-red carpeting at the top that leads to a vast, sinister-looking underground room within a cavern. There are pews like in a church and an altar, and dominating all this is a throne of skulls—on which no one sits.

You enter the huge room and, mesmerized, walk toward the empty throne.

"Let us begin today by welcoming our visitors," a thunderous voice bellows at the living dead that are

Turn to the next page.

now in the gigantic room with you. They are filing down the aisles and slowly filling the pews. Their luminous eyes are fixed straight ahead.

"Welcome," intone the dead sitting in the pews, their voices as one.

"Let them join us in the magic of death!" The words seem to thunder from the throne, but there is still no one there.

"Who are you?" you demand, your words rendered into a feeble, barely audible whisper by your mounting terror.

"The one who frightens you most, and whom you understand the least!" is the booming answer.

"Who?" you beg.

There is laughter. And then you scream. Though you remain standing between Shawn and Tanya, sitting on the throne of skulls is your exact double!

"That's not me!" you cry.

"I *am* you," says your duplicate in your voice. "But for others it is someone else." The voice of your duplicate changes to a boy's voice—to *Shawn's* voice. And then it is Shawn sitting on the throne of skulls. The laughter rises in pitch, and becomes a girl's laugh—*Tanya's* laugh—as Shawn's face changes into hers.

"Stop it!" you scream.

"As you wish," says the Tanya look-alike. And

Turn to the ***next page.***

with that the flesh on her face slips off like some horrid, semiliquid mask, revealing a face of bone. As the flesh slides off the rest of the body, other transformations take place. Skin regrows on the face, then on the body. Clothing is replaced as well, and soon, sitting on the throne, is a handsome, dark-haired young man in an old-fashioned, double-breasted suit.

"I hope my looks meet with your approval," he says, smiling. "It's nice to have visitors. Haven't had any for over a year, but three or four hundred years ago, I had visitors by the dozens."

"Wh-who are you?" you stammer. "I mean, *what* are you?"

"I am Vlad Tepes. However, the peasants around you, to whom I gave the gift of everlasting life, of living death, refer to me ungraciously as—"

"Dracula!" cries Tanya.

"Very good, young lady. I am Dracula, or as some like to call me, the Prince of Darkness."

"Please," you beg. "Please let us leave."

"Of course," answers Dracula. "But not before I give you your gift."

"We don't want anything from a vampire!" you cry.

"Not even that lovely ring on your finger?"

You feel something on your finger, even before you hold up your left hand to stare at the gold band

Turn to the next page.

with the black stone on your ring finger. You pull on it, but find it is now like part of your flesh!

"Let's get out of here," whispers Shawn. "This guy is—"

"There are worse places to be," interrupts Dracula. He laughs as his face becomes translucent, followed by his entire body. *Inside* him, behind the window that is now his flesh, there are bats crawling, flying, or hanging upside down.

Suddenly he opens his mouth . . . and in a constant, seemingly endless stream, thousands of the horrid creatures fly out. The cavern erupts in a cacophony of their shrieks, mixing with flapping wings. The air fills with the black monsters as they continue to emerge from Dracula's mouth, streaming out in a horrid, airborne parade. Then as the last bat escapes, the terrible vampire closes its mouth, and the audience—the congregation of corpses—laughs, their horrid giggles rising to a crescendo—into an insane, high-pitched howl of delight.

As the bats circle in their frenzy of flight, the three of you try to run, but the corpses converge on you and push you to the dark-red carpet. You try to rise but find yourself held by their bloodless hands. But what is worse, you see a shrieking black whirlwind of bats descending upon you. They swarm all

Turn to the next page.

over you, their wings slapping your face, their claws grabbing at your skin. Then just as their hollow, serrated fangs sink into the flesh of your neck, your eyes grow heavy and everything goes dim.

Perhaps a moment passes . . . perhaps an hour . . . or is it a year? Your eyes slowly open. You are sitting in one of the pews, the living corpses of Shawn and Tanya to either side of you, the ceiling of the place a dense mass of sleeping bats suspended upside down in hundreds of rows. And on his throne, an oversized bat perched on his shoulder, is Dracula . . . in the middle of some kind of speech.

". . . and thusly," he says in a grand voice, "we learn of the dark joys of life within death and death within life, for therein lies the key to . . ."

As he drones on, you look at your friends. The three of you smile at each other, then return your attention to Dracula, enraptured by his words, enthralled by his presence, pleased to be in his morbid congregation. He is your master now, as you settle into a never-ending, lifeless existence of mindless servitude.

You head into the dark tunnel and soon find it opening up into a broad cave with a ceiling so low the three of you have to walk bent over. Trudging along in a stoop, you notice a strong, musky aroma.

"What's that weird smell?" asks Shawn.

"Some sort of animal, I think," you say, noticing paw prints and droppings.

Hunched over, you make your way through the cave and out a narrow, sunlit opening. The three of you stretch your muscles, glad to be out of the low-ceilinged cave and able to stand up straight. You gaze at the landscape below. At your feet is a short, rocky incline and beyond that is a seemingly endless expanse of pine forest.

"It's beautiful!" exclaims Shawn.

"Let's go!" says Tanya enthusiastically.

In a happy mood, the three of you pick your way down a slope of loose shale. Taking in the view and moving at a very leisurely pace, you suddenly realize that you're lagging behind your friends. "Wait up!" you say with a laugh . . . as suddenly your feet go out from under you. Letting out a yelp, tumbling face-forward, you try to break your fall with your hands, but slam headfirst into the gnarled stump of a tree.

For a moment the world goes dark . . . and then you feel someone shaking you.

Turn to the next page.

"You OK?" asks Tanya, kneeling over you.

"Yeah," you mumble, as Shawn helps you sit up. You rub a knot on your head and feel a wave of dizziness, which quickly passes.

"You really took a tumble," says Tanya.

"Head hurt?" asks Shawn.

"Nah, not really," you say. "Just a bump on the old noggin." Forcing a smile and taking Shawn's hand, you pull yourself to your feet.

"Want to go back to the cave?" asks Tanya.

"No, really, I'm fine," you say, heading off down a path of yellow grass through green forest. "Come on!"

Soon the three of you come to a creek, where two cute bear cubs are frisking about. You and your friends smile at their antics but then continue on down the trail, knowing it is not wise being near the cubs for long. The mother bear is probably not too far away, and if she were to have the slightest feeling her babies were in danger, she might attack.

As if your worst fears are coming true, suddenly a hulking, brown-gray bear streaks out from the woods. Your eyes open wide with horror at the ferocious creature, as you are transfixed by its sudden appearance, its size, its speed. The bear's silver-tipped fur glistens in the sun, and its huge shoulders make a hump along her back.

Turn to the ***next page.***

Knowing that running from the beast is impossible, the three of you back away, stumbling on slick pine needles.

The bear stops in its tracks and paws at the ground, as if deciding who to attack first. Snarling, with flecks of foam dribbling from its mouth, the beast roars, then charges . . . straight at Shawn.

Completely bowled over, Shawn staggers to his feet and tries to get away, but the beast wraps him in a deadly embrace.

Suddenly Shawn pulls an arm free and delivers a powerful, looping blow to the bear's forehead, causing it to lose its grip and to stumble sideways, like a punch-drunk boxer. The beast bellows, comes at Shawn again, and smashes him on the side of the head with a vicious swipe of its terrible claws. Shawn goes flying, and lands with a *crack* against the thick root of a tree jutting out from an eroded bank.

You are about to rush to where he lies on his back with his hand to the bloodied side of his face, but a bellow of rage from the bear stops you. Turning around, you see it charging Tanya. Desperately trying to protect your friend, you lunge at Tanya and throw her to the ground, then twist sideways as the bear rushes past. It skids to a halt, then turns and leaps at you. A monstrous clawed paw slashes across

Turn to the next page.

your shoulder, knocking you to the ground.

For a moment you black out. As you come to, you hear a crunching noise that sounds like a dog gnawing on a steak bone. Then to your horror, you see what the crunching noise really is.

Shawn is lying facedown and unconscious. The bear—probably weighing eight hundred pounds—is on top of him, tearing at one of his arms. Tanya, hefting a heavy branch and shrieking hysterically, lunges at the bear and hits its back. The bear roars in fury, wheels on her, and slashes at her with outstretched claws. As one blow hits her, she is knocked backward, tumbling down out of sight over an embankment. The bear then returns its attention to Shawn.

Nauseated, with rubbery legs, you stagger to your feet and grab a stone. With a yell, you jump onto the bear's back, slamming the stone into its neck and head. You draw blood, but your efforts do little more than enrage the beast further. It lets out a chilling roar, then rolls over onto you. You feel your wrist snap and the stone fall from your hand.

Somehow you find yourself on your knees, then weakly you lurch to your feet. The bear is only inches from your face. It snarls and wraps monster arms around you, crushing you to its chest. It lets out an almost human scream . . . and razor-sharp claws are

Turn to the next page.

slashing at you. Over and over it slices your flesh, tearing at every part of you.

Shrieking with pain, you stumble backward, wiping at the blood coursing down your face. Then you grab a branch and stab at the giant creature as you try to get away.

But the bear merely slaps the branch from your hands, then charges again. Snarling and snapping, it throws its entire weight into you, and together you crash to the ground.

It's all over, a voice inside your head wails, as you and your giant foe roll over and over on the ground. All breath is knocked from your body. You feel your ribs cracking, huge teeth and claws tearing into you. The pain is excruciating, beyond belief. Your mind begins to spin, and you black out.

And then you feel someone shaking you.

"You OK?" asks Tanya anxiously.

"Yeah," you mumble as Shawn helps you sit up. You rub a knot on your head and feel a wave of dizziness, which quickly passes.

For an instant, bits and pieces of the horrific dream filter through your mind. But then it fades, and you can remember nothing of it.

"You were coming down the hill," says Shawn, "down from the cave. Guess you weren't looking

*Turn to the **next page**.*

where you were going, because you sure took a fall."

"Yeah, you really smacked your head hard against that gnarled tree stump," adds Tanya. "Knocked you out cold for a minute." She frowns.

"Head hurt?" asks Shawn.

"Nah, not really," you say. "Just a bump on the noggin." Forcing a smile and taking Shawn's hand, you pull yourself to your feet.

"Want to go back to the cave?" asks Tanya.

"No, I'm fine," you say, heading off down a path of yellow grass through a green forest. "Come on!"

Soon, the three of you come to a creek where two cute bear cubs are frisking about. You and your friends smile at their antics, then continue on down the trail. . . .

Then a thought snaps into your consciousness. You have been here before, done this before, said the same things . . . *before*. And you know what will happen next.

Suddenly a hulking, brown-gray bear streaks out from the woods . . .

Just
when you
thought
it was safe
to fall
asleep . . .

. . . Watch out for these other

NIGHTMARES!
HOW WILL YOURS END?

titles: